A
Merrie
Prairie
Christmas

From Doyle - Christmas 1989

A Merrie Prairie Christmas
Carl H. Wichman, editor

© Prairie House Inc. 1989. All rights reserved.

ISBN 0-911007-13-X
Library of Congress data pending.

First printing 1989

Prairie House
Box 9199
Fargo ND 58106-9199

For more information on books by the authors included in A
Merrie Prairie Christmas — and other regional literature of
the Upper Midwest — write for the entire Prairie House
catalog.

Cover illustration: Gary Baune

A Merrie Prairie Christmas

Holiday Memories, Tales and Traditions from the Dakotas and Minnesota

Carl H. Wichman, editor

PRAIRIE HOUSE

Table of Contents

Christmases Present

Christmas in the Kitchen

Christmas on the Lighter Side

Introduction

We cover the territory with stories from favorite authors — new as well as old: from the ranches of the Dakotas to the lakes of the Minnesota northwoods, from a South Dakota farmhouse to a cozy living room in Fargo, North Dakota.

The traditions of our forefathers handed down to us are retold in the stories of "Der Nikolaus is Coming" (Germany), "Julebuk" (Norway) and "The Story of the Christmas Rose" (Swedish). The St. Lucia Day tradition of December 13 is explained, from its customs to its often-surprising source.

Frances Wold's "The Silver Ornaments" and Susan Hauser's "The Finest Gifts" bring forth cherished memories of that favorite ornament — carefully unpacked each year from its padded surroundings to hang on the special Christmas tree that Jack Zaleski writes about in "Of Christmas Memories and Fragrant Trees."

We all have memories of the great smells of Christmas baking. Some of these can be relived in our *Christmas in the Kitchen* section. A couple of the stories included here come complete with recipes handed down from authors Andrea Halgrimson and Susan Hauser to *your* family. Gwen Petersen sheds a humorous light on the art of keeping your sanity during the holiday cooking crunch.

If you're looking for a story to make you think about what Christmas is really all about, turn to *Keeping Christ in Christmas*. It's a nice diversion from the commercial rush so many of us experience and reaffirms the story of why this holiday (or "holy" day) is celebrated.

If history is your passion, we've got it. In *Christmases Past* we learn of historical Christmases, both real and imagined. If you grew up in a one-room school or just about any rural setting, the memories of veteran teachers shared in "Country Schools at Christmas" should ring a bell. To find out how the first white arrivals celebrated the season in the Upper Midwest, turn to "Early North Dakota Christmases."

For a more recent look at winter, turn to *Christmases Present*. For those of you who have spent one or more Christmases on the northern plains, you can easily relate to the stories of "A Northern Christmas" and "But Baby It's Cold Outside: Memories of Minnesota Winters."

Humorous holiday glimpses, multiple views of Santa Claus, and a Christmas mystery round out *A Merrie Prairie Christmas*.

Not only are these fun to read and excellently penned — they also bring back an unending flow of memories of past Christmases. Hopefully there will be a story or two that will become a tradition for your family to share year after year.

I wish everyone who reads this collection
A MERRIE PRAIRIE CHRISTMAS.

— Carl H. Wichman
Editor

Christmases
Past

Hannah

Laura French

This story takes place somewhere in the Red River Valley, sometime in the late 1800s. Although the people, places, and events are imaginary, I hope that this story is true.

Winter was late in coming that year. Through all of October and well into November, days were shirt-sleeve warm and at night only a thin layer of ice formed on the top of the watering tanks.

For Hannah Manning, the lone teacher in the township's one-room school, the warm weather was a blessing. With no howling winds to struggle against, no deep snow drifts to wade through, the dozen younger children, aged five to twelve, could make the four- or five-mile trip to and from school easily.

On the other hand, the five older children, aged fourteen to seventeen, were rarely in school. Every fine autumn day could be better used in the farmyard than in the schoolhouse.

That arrangement was fine with Hannah. The little children were her pets. The best part of her job was sharing their excitement as they learned to read and write and do their sums. But with the older children, Hannah was always nervously aware that her own eleventh-grade education wasn't much better than theirs.

Already Jan Bjork had begun to move ahead of her in mathematics. At seventeen, Jan was only three years younger than Hannah, and he was nearly a foot taller. Soon he'd be noticeably smarter in math — and then how could she hold his respect?

Fifteen-year-old Libby Eriksdottir was Hannah's other problem student. In the past year, she'd begun asking lively questions about American history for which Hannah often had no answers.

Hannah studied hard on her own. Still, she knew that wasn't enough. The way things were wasn't fair to the students or to her. That's why Hannah had come up with a secret plan. Not even the Widow Jenkins, with whom Hannah boarded, knew about it. Hannah was going to college! The following fall, she would enroll in the brand-new Moorhead Normal School.

There, she could learn more about literature and history and mathematics — and she could learn to be a better teacher. After she graduated, she could come back to Oscar Township, or maybe even go on to a better school in a bigger town.

Within a few months, Hannah would have to reveal her secret plan. The school board would have to find a replacement. The children would have to get used to the idea that a new teacher would be coming the fall. Hannah's heart felt heavy when she thought about it. In three years of teaching, she'd grown to love her students. She didn't look forward to saying goodbye.

The last day of the two-month fall term felt to Hannah like practice for the final goodbye. More for her sake than theirs, she reminded them that she'd see them again when the winter term started in February. She had to force herself to smile as she stood at the schoolhouse door and wished her students a happy Thanksgiving.

The day after Thanksgiving dawned bright and cold. Hannah looked out her bedroom window at a changed landscape. The long autumn was finally over. The snow that was on the ground would stay until spring.

Ordinarily, Hannah welcomed the break between school terms. But this year was different. Without the everyday noise and distraction of the schoolroom, her secret weighed heavily.

One minute she felt so eager to get on with her life that she wished she could leave for Moorhead immediately. The next minute she'd feel terrified of leaving and wonder if she shouldn't drop the idea all together.

The warring feelings started to tell on Hannah's nerves. On the Monday after Thanksgiving, she burned a batch of cookies and chipped one of Mrs. Jenkins' prized figurines while dusting it.

Finally, Hannah excused herself and went to her room. There, she read the same page in her history book three times without taking in a word of it. She closed the book, walked to her dressing table, and sat down to give the reflection in the mirror a good talking to. "This has to stop," she said. "Widow Jenkins was giving you a suspicious look. If you can't act normally, she'll know you have something up your sleeve."

In the mirror, Hannah's gray eyes looked helplessly back at her. "How can I act normally?" they seemed to be asking.

Hannah stared back at her reflection. Her lips drew together in a look of determination. "Make yourself useful," she said. "Get involved in a project."

The gray eyes still looked helplessly back at her. She was being vague, she knew. "Christmas," she said desperately. "This will be your last Christmas in Oscar Township. Make it a special one. Make gifts for all the children. Make gifts for everyone in town."

The eyes looked pained. Sewing and fancywork were not Hannah's favorite past times. Making a hundred gifts would be torture.

"It also wouldn't keep your mind occupied," Hannah told her reflection. "Still, the idea of giving everyone a gift is a good one. If only there were a way to make a gift by using my mind, instead of my hands."

A Merrie Prairie Christmas

Suddenly, the eyes grew round. "There is a way!" she exclaimed. "I can give a gift to all of Oscar Township. It will be a special gift, too — one that everyone will remember for a long, long time!"

Hannah jumped up from her dressing table and ran downstairs. "Oh, Mrs. Jenkins," she exclaimed, "I've just had the most wonderful idea!"

Hannah found the Widow Jenkins in the kitchen, mixing a batch of gingerbread. "I've had the most wonderful idea," she repeated. "I want to put on a Christmas pageant. All of the children will take part, and the entire township will be invited."

Widow Jenkins stopped stirring the gingerbread and smiled.

Encouraged by the smile, Hannah quickly outlined the program. "We'll start with an instrumental selection — perhaps Pehr Olafson would play 'Oh Little Town of Bethlehem' on the violin. After that, we'll enact the Christmas story. Jan Bjork can read from the Bible, and the younger children, all in costume, will act out the parts. Then, finally, we'll have a community sing." Hannah clapped her hands delightedly as another idea occurred to her. "Santa Claus! We could have Santa Claus come with gifts for all the children. Mr. Rystad would be perfect for the part!"

Widow Jenkin's smile had disappeared as Hannah spoke. "That's very ambitious for a first pageant, " she said. "The carols are nice, and of course we must have the Christmas story. But perhaps Jan could simply read it with the younger children gathered around him."

"That would be no better than staying home!" Hannah protested. "It won't be so difficult, really — you forget how much energy children have! Besides, we have nearly three weeks to prepare."

The next morning, Hannah bundled up and set off to inform her performers of the parts she'd assigned to them.

Pehr readily agreed to play the violin. Jan needed some coaxing, but at last he agreed to read the Christmas story. Libby said she'd be happy to be the angel. Other children eagerly signed on as shepherds, Magi and the Holy Family. Little Peder Nygaard volunteered to bring his pet goat to add reality to the manger scene. Smiling, Hannah said she'd think about it. She left the visit to Mr. Rystad for another day. Telling someone he reminded you of Santa Claus had to be done tactfully, and Hannah wanted to sure she was up to it.

Hannah had set the first rehearsal for the following Monday, and she was at the schoolhouse bright and early to build a fire in the stove and pull the desk into the corner, leaving the front of the room for a stage. "We'll need some decorations to make the room Christmasy," she said aloud. "I'll ask Jan about cutting some trees when he arrives."

But Jan never did arrive. "Pa made him stay home to help finish the addition to the granary," his younger sister Karla said.

"He can't afford to miss many more practices," she told the Widow Jenkins that evening. "His father knew about the pageant — how rude of him to make Jan bother with the silly old granary."

"I don't think it's silly, " Widow Jenkins said. "Jan's father and mother came to this county within a year or two of Mr. Jenkins and me. That was back in the 1860s, when this land was nothing but sky and prairie. I remember years when the snows came in October, and we all went hungry before spring. I remember when farmers worked all summer, blazing sun and soaking rain, to get ten or fifteen acres plowed and planted, and each year another acre or two broken to the plow." Widow Jenkins paused, perhaps to let her words sink into Hannah's mind, or perhaps to honor unspoken memories of those years.

"Now, twenty-five years later, the results of all that hard work are starting to show," Widow Jenkins continued. "Farmer Bjork can grow enough to get his family through the winter. By next year, he'll even be able to put grain by so that one bad crop won't mean famine. That's why the granary seems so important, Hannah. Mr. Bjork is building for the future."

"But so am I!" Hannah countered. "Real progress isn't just a bigger harvest. It's making a better life — one with time for education and culture. That's what this pageant is all about."

Widow Jenkins nodded. "I appreciate what you're doing," she said. "But it won't be any easier for you to bring your kind of culture here than it was for us to bring agriculture."

Over the next few weeks, Widow Jenkins' words proved all too true. Jan continued to miss rehearsals. Pehr came to rehearsals, but it was clear that he wasn't finding much time to practice his violin solo. The rasp of the bow at times made Hannah's eyes water. The children in the pageant, who were so lithe and agile as they ran through the fields, somehow turned to clumsy oafs when they had to take two steps across the stage.

The one bright spot so far was Mr. Rystad, who had happily agreed to play Santa Claus. "I can't imagine why you picked me, though," he teased, patting his ample belly. "Why not Erik Mobraaten?"

"He doesn't have your twinkling eyes," Hannah had teased back — not mentioning that Mobraaten also weighed at least a hundred pounds less than the ample Mr. Rystad.

Three days before the pageant, the Widow Jenkins finished the last of the costumes. "They're beautiful," Hannah breathed as Mrs. Jenkins held them up one by one. The shepherds' robes were made from burlap that the widow had scrubbed to softness in lye soap. Mary's dress, made of store-bought blue cloth, was soft and flowing.

A Merrie Prairie Christmas

Best of all, in Hannah's mind, were the Magi's robes. They were pieced together from many different colors and kinds of cloth. The result, though, wasn't rag-tag at all. "They look so colorful and ... exotic," Hannah said. "The children will love 'em."

The children didn't love them at all. The girl who was playing Mary announced that the flowing blue robe looked like a nightgown. But her scorn was mild compared to that of the three Magi. "That's a dress!" Lars Langfeld said. "I'm not going to stand up here in front of everybody in a dress!"

"Me either," his two fellow Magi echoed.

Hannah insisted that a robe was not really a dress. She coaxed the boys to look at the rich colors in the costumes. She even dragged them to the big illustrated Bible at the back of the school room and showed them the similar garments worn by the prophets and the kings of Egypt and even by Jesus and his apostles. It was no use. The boys stubbornly insisted that they would not wear dresses. Either they would play the Magi wearing their comfortable bib overalls, or Hannah could find some girls who were willing to take their parts.

Hannah struggled to hold her temper. What more could she expect? These boys had been raised to believe that the only education they needed was in handling a team of oxen and a plow. If they were ever to learn anything more, it was up to her to teach them. "At least until spring. After that, I can go study among people who appreciate the finer things in life," she thought.

It was that thought, more than anything — the knowledge that the trials of Oscar Township were only temporary — that kept Hannah from screaming at the boys. Instead, she calmly called an end to the rehearsal for the day. "We'll all sleep on it, and tomorrow we'll decide what to do," she said.

When the children had been bundled up against the cold and sent on their way, Hannah remained behind, carefully folding the hated costumes and wondering what she would say to the Widow Jenkins. Lost in thought, she was startled by the knock on the door.

It was Olav Granrud, the president of the school board. His refusal to meet her glance told her there was trouble. "Rehearsing for the pageant," he said. It wasn't a question, and Hannah didn't answer. "I've heard about the pageant. I've heard you're going to have Santa Claus." Hannah remained silent.

"We can't have that," Mr. Granrud said. "There are parents in this district who don't let their kids know about Santa. They think it's sacrilege."

"Santa has been part of Christmas for hundreds of years. It's tradition!" Hannah countered.

"It's not everyone's tradition," Mr. Granrud said. "But it is everyone's school district. Make your choice — no Santa, or no pageant."

Hannah stared at the school board president in amazement. She was clutching one of the scorned Magi robes. It seemed somehow to give her courage. "Mr. Granrud, my idea was to give this pageant as a gift to the people of Oscar Township. The idea has brought me nothing but trouble.

"For two weeks, I have put up with the narrow-mindedness of adults and children who are opposed to anything new, anything exciting, anything the least bit civilized. It is clear to me now, finally, that you and the other citizens of the township don't want my gift. I will not force it on you."

Hannah snatched her coat, bonnet, and muff off the hook where they were hanging and pulled them on as she continued to speak: "You ask me to choose between two alternatives. I say to you, Mr. Granrud, that you may have them both: No Santa and no pageant." She paused at the door of the schoolhouse. "I will even offer you a bonus you hadn't bargained for: No teacher."

Hannah opened the door, stepped outside, and slammed the door shut behind her.

After Hannah stormed out of her meeting with Mr. Granrud, she marched down the schoolhouse path without looking back. Her mind was a blind, blank rage. It was only after several minutes that she was even able to form angry thoughts: "How dare he interfere with the pageant! At this late date, too, when the costumes are all made and everything is nearly ready."

Honesty forced Hannah to admit that the pageant was not so "nearly ready" as all that — but that simply rechanneled her anger without quenching it. "The whole idea was a terrible mistake. These — these farmers aren't capable of appreciating culture or education. They want their daughters to be able to read the seed catalogs and their sons to be able to calculate what they'll get for their crops.

"Strong back and weak minds — that's what they want for the next generation. Well, I'm not having any of it!"

Hannah decided that she would leave Oscar Township immediately — that day. She had a married sister in Traill County with whom she could stay for the balance of the year. Or maybe, she thought, a ray of hope brightening her black thoughts, the Moorhead Normal School would let her begin her studies mid-year.

Needing more time to think, Hannah followed a path that branched off the road to Mrs. Jenkins' house. The path, which led across Hendrup Prairie, was one she often walked in summer. At the far end of the prairie was a small pond around which grew a dense stand of wild blueberries. In winter, however, the path was little traveled. The

16   *A Merrie Prairie Christmas*

settlers taught their children that evil trolls inhabited the prairies during the winter — trolls who would boil the children in a pot and eat them for dinner.

"No one thinks that tradition is sacrilege," Hannah said out loud. Without a wagon rut to walk in, Hannah was suddenly aware that she'd left her boots back at the schoolhouse. A gust of wind tugged at her coat and wrapped her petticoats around her legs, making it difficult to take a step forward.

Hannah shivered and glanced over her shoulder at the main road. Perhaps she should turn back, she thought — but no. She needed time to calm down. Hannah took a deep breath and moved on.

The wind picked up, but Hannah struggled against it and kept walking. When she was halfway across the prairie and could see the line of trees and shrubs along the lakeshore, she felt the first snowflake hit her face. Looking up, she saw a swirl of white, as if a feather ticking were being emptied from the sky. In seconds, the swirl engulfed her.

Hannah turned and looked back. She could see nothing but endless whiteness. There was no sign of the main road. Ahead, if she squinted, she could barely make out the outline of trees along the lake. She must go on. The trees would provide some shelter until the storm died. Hannah felt fear leap into her heart as she realized that storms often lasted for hours — sometimes even for days!

She wouldn't think of that — in fact, she discovered, she couldn't think of that. It took all of her effort to keep moving against the storm. At times, the line of trees was invisible in the snow. She could only hope she was still on the path; her feet were now too numb to tell the difference between snow-covered path and snow-covered prairie.

The wind let up for a brief moment and visibility improved. Hannah saw, to her dismay, that the line of trees was now off to her right. She had strayed badly from the path. She straightened her course as best she could. Then the wind picked up again and the trees were lost in a veil of whiteness.

Hannah struggled on, seemingly for hours. Then, suddenly, a black shape loomed in the darkness. Hannah's small scream was lost in the noise of the wind. Embarassment mingled with relief as she realized it was a tree, not a troll. She stumbled to the tree and hugged it unashamedly. A few more steps forward, and she was sheltered by the fringe of trees and bushes along the lakeshore. For a moment, out of the wind, Hannah felt warmer. Soon, however, the cold assailed her again.

She tried to break some boughs off an evergreen tree, but the frozen needles stripped off in a shower like summer rain. Finally, she crawled as deeply as she could into a cluster of blueberry bushes and sat, curled into a ball with her chin on her knees.

The cold was seeping into her brain, making it slow and groggy. Somewhere, far away, her feet were aching, but it didn't seem to matter anymore. Soon, she knew, she would go to sleep, never to wake up. That didn't seem to matter, either.

Except ... except for the children. It was sad that she wouldn't be able to say goodby. Would they miss her, she wondered? Yes — yes, of course, they would. They had liked her. Dreamily, she remembered the schoolhouse. As she worked with one child, another would call to her, "Teacher!" She would go to help that child, and soon yet another would call out, "Teacher! Teacher!"

It seemed as though she could hear the voices. They sounded almost real. Hannah raised her head. The vision of the schoolhouse vanished, but the calls remained. "Teacher! Teacher!"

They were real! "I'm here!" Hannah shouted. "I'm here!"

Huddled in the bushes, unable to see even the lakeshore a few feet away, Hannah cried for help with her last remaining strength. Then she fell once again into a dreamy half-sleep. She was dimly aware of someone shouting, "Here she is! Over here!"

She felt herself being lifted into something that seemed to be a wood sled. That was fitting, she thought, for someone as stiff and cold as a tree.

In the sled, she was bumped and jostled along the path. She wished that the jostling would stop. All she wanted to do was sleep ... sleep.

But how could she sleep with all that light in her eyes? She woke, blinking in the sunlight. Gradually she opened her eyes and discovered that she was in her own bedroom in Widow Jenkins' house! "Was it all a dream?" she wondered. The throbbing ache in her feet told her that it had been all too real.

Just then the door opened and the widow herself walked in. "Well, well, awake at last!" she said. Her voice sounded cheerful, but her face looked haggard.

"How long did I sleep?" Hannah asked.

"Nearly a day and a half," the widow replied.

Hannah gasped and sat up. "Then this is December twenty-third!" she exclaimed. "The pageant ...." She sank back against the pillows. There was no pageant. "No Santa Claus, no pageant, and no teacher." The words echoed in her mind.

"This is not time for worry," the widow said. "You just be grateful that you're alive, and with all your fingers and toes. If the children hadn't found you when they did" — she broke off, shaking her head.

"How did they find me?" Hannah asked.

"They'd gone to the schoolhouse — apparently to apologize for ... something. When you weren't there, they headed over here. When I told them you weren't her, either, they retraced their steps, and saw your tracks starting across the prairie," Widow Jenkins said. "They ran to the Langfeld place and got some baling twine. Jan and three of the others tied the twine around their waists, and Karla Bjork stayed in the road, playing out the twine so they'd be able to find their way back."

"They were very smart," Hannah said. "Much smarter than I was."

Widow Jenkins departed without another word.

Hannah was left to think — about music and literature and life and death, about culture and about courage. What she concluded was that she was glad she'd already resigned from Oscar Township school, because she didn't see how she could ever face the children again. Then she dozed off.

When she awoke, another day had passed. She was feeling considerably better; even the dull ache in her feet had lessened overnight. In the afternoon, the Widow Jenkins came in with a newly knitted pair of slippers — enormous slippers big enough to fit over the bandages on Hannah's feet. Hannah burst out laughing when she saw the two huge, blue, fuzzy lumps at the ends of her ankles.

Widow Jenkins nodded solemnly and said, "They'll do." Then she went to the wardrobe and pulled out Hannah's best blue dress. "You'd best get ready," she said. "I have a feeling we may have company this evening."

Hannah's heart gave a thump. "Mr. Granrud," she thought, "come to finish our 'discussion.'" She might as well face up to it. With a sigh, she shifted to the edge of the bed and, slightly giddy, rose to her feet.

It took Hannah a long time to get ready. She was just putting up her hair when the widow called, "Hannah, dear, company!" She stood up and walked clumsily down the stairs in her bandaged feet.

At the foot of the stairs, she gasped. Widow Jenkins' house had been transformed! Balsam garlands draped every window and doorway. Candles glowed on every vacant surface. There were few vacant surfaces, however; it seemed as though all of Oscar Township was crowded into the widow's house. Grown-ups sat and stood in the hallway and in the dining room and kitchen. In the parlor, in addition to a tree that nearly touched the ceiling, there were the children.

Libby Eriksdottir stepped forward. "Sit here, teacher," she said, leading Hannah to a vacant chair at the front of the crowd. When Hannah was settled, Libby cleared her throat and said importantly, "Our first entertainment this evening will be Pehr Olafson playing the violin."

Pehr stepped forward, hair slicked down and cheeks shining with shy excitement. He tucked the violin under his chin and began to play "Oleanna," a rousing Norwegian folk song.

Hannah suppressed a smile. It wasn't as Christmasy as "O Little Town of Bethlehem," but it was much more pleasant to listen to.

After Pehr fled the room to escape the crowd's warm applause, Libby announced, "Now Jan Bjork will read the Christmas story."

Jan sat down on the hearth and opened the Bible. The little children gathered around him. "And it came to pass in those days, that there went out a decree from Caesar Augustus, that all the world should be taxed," he began. He voice was deep and sure. The little children, who idolized Jan, listened to the story as though for the first time. For everyone in that quiet, pine-scented house, the story seemed brand-new.

There was a long pause at the end of the story, and then Libby said, "We will now sing carols."

The Widow Jenkins' piano was put to good use, with carols sung in English and Norwegian and Swedish and German. When the last note of "Silent Night" had faded away, there was a sudden, startling jangle of sleigh bells outside. That was followed by a hearty "Ho, ho, ho!"

Karla Bjork shouted what Hannah had been thinking: "Santa Claus!"

Sure enough, the door opened and through the crowd came a jolly, portly figure in a red suit with white eyebrows and white whiskers. The children gathered around, laughing and shouting.

With all the attention on the children, no one noticed when Mr. Granrud separated himself from the crowd and came to stand next to Hannah. "A person can have a change of heart," he told her.

"Yes," she said quietly, "a person can."

She knew, then, that her job would be waiting for her when the winter term began in February. Sometime soon after that, she would have to tell Mr. Granrud that, come spring, she'd be leaving. When she really did leave, however, it wouldn't be in anger. Nor would it be forever.

Most important, she wouldn't leave believing that college was the only place for learning. The children and adults of Oscar Township had taught her a lesson that she'd cherish and remember for as long as she lived.

Laura French: "Hannah." Originally published in *The Forum of Fargo-Moorhead*, December 1987.

Dakota Winter Memories

Frances Wold

Sometimes as I listen to the furnace hum reassuringly through these long winter days, or as I turn on the electric blanket before crawling into bed, I remember other days when keeping warm was not just a matter of turning up a thermostat or pressing a button.

As I allow my mind to ramble a bit, I recall sights and sounds and scents that bring those times into sharp focus — memories that are common to all who grew up in North Dakota before electricity came to the prairies, and when "horse power" meant just that.

Do you remember....

The smell of woolens drying in the warm oven.... The steely chill of the pump handle on a winter evening.... Picking frozen eggs from the nests in the chicken house.... The cheery jingling of sleigh bells as teams went by on the road.... The heavenly aroma of fresh bread when you arrived home from school....

Shoveling the path to the outhouse, and probably having to shovel off the seat, too.... The arctic air in a country schoolhouse on Monday morning....

A winter funeral, with the grave dug by hand in earth frozen six feet deep.... The excruciating itch of chilblained feet.... Wrestling frozen overalls and sheets into the house from the clothesline....

Buttoned leggings.... Toasting your toes on the nickel-plated fender of the baseburner.... Melting snow for Saturday night baths.... Breaking the ice in the kitchen water pail before you could make the breakfast coffee.... Hitching your sled behind a bobsled for a free ride.... Popping corn in an iron skillet on the kitchen range.... Coal slack, clinkers and ashes....

Taking a hot flat iron to bed with you to keep your feet warm.... Playing "Rook" by the light of a kerosene lamp.... Banking the house....

Your mother putting mustard plasters on your chest.... The bulges your long underwear made under your black, ribbed stockings....

Setting your mother's house plants on chairs by the stove each night to keep them from freezing.... Putting the car up on blocks the first of November....

Piling the family into a bobsled to go to a "house party".... Climbing the icy steps of the windmill to oil the gears.... Filling the lantern before evening chores.... The time the soot in the chimney caught on fire.... The eerie wail of a coyote floating over snow covered fields.... Fresh pork and sauerkraut?

Memories of Dakota winters...some good, some not so pleasant. Would you want to relive them?

Frances Wold: "North Dakota Winter Memories." From *Prairie Scrapbook*. Frances Wold, 1980.

Country Schools at Christmas

Bonnie Hughes Falk, editor

A Christmas program was a *must*. We started practicing right after Thanksgiving. We'd hand out the parts to be memorized before Thanksgiving vacation. It was indeed fun to get ready for the "big night." We had to provide a stage, using sheets as curtains. One neighbor would bring a gas lantern for light. Then the last day planks were brought in for extra seating. The fathers were good helpers. The parents brought the lunch and plenty of coffee. When the program and lunch were over, the desks were pushed to the side and the planks were removed. Then, young and old played games and everyone enjoyed themselves.

— *Selma O. Sanvik*

The Christmas program was the highlight of the year, rivaled only in importance by the annual school picnic or the visit of the county superintendent. The country school programs were exciting times, both for the child and the parents. Each child always gave a recitation or had a part in a play involving several students. The front of the room was closed off from the admiring audience by and old, much-mended, gray curtain, which was strung by strong wire.

After the program, lunch of hearty meat sandwiches and large pieces of cake was served by the mothers. A bushel basket full of tin cups would be borrowed from an auctioneer for the big celebration at school, and coffee was brought in large gray enamel coffee pots by wives of school board members. The balance of the evening was spent playing games or dancing reels. This part of the evening was much enjoyed by older students and visitors.

— *Margaret Seeger Hedlund*

At Christmas you were expected to put on a program for parents and the community. We strung up a curtain across the front of the room, and behind it we tried to have order out of chaos, with all the children, properties, and everything back there. Usually it turned out reasonably well. I always hated all the time it took to practice for those programs because we lost good school time. But it was expected, and often a teacher was judged by the programs she produced.

— *Helen C. Williams*

There was always a Christmas program at school put on by the teacher and pupils and attended by nearly everyone. Some programs were given in the afternoon. If the programs were given at night, the families would bring their lanterns and lamps to light up the school building. Along with the program, there was always a lunch. Then we got back into the horse-drawn bobsleigh and headed for home, listening to the ringing of the sleigh bells.

— *Forrest and Ethelyn McKinley*

During the Christmas season we spent much of our time practicing for our annual Christmas program. We spent hours cutting out red and green wreaths to use to decorate all the windows. This was always such a happy time. Everyone was in the holiday spirit, and we got to know all of our fellow students so well during this time. All of the students took part in decorating the Christmas tree, which was always placed at the side of the stage, along with a manger scene.

At the end of the program, we had a pot luck lunch, which included sandwiches and cake. Sometimes we had a basket social. It was always fun to see who bought our baskets.

— *Van Johnson*

I remember practicing for our Christmas program from Thanksgiving on. On the night of the performance, the sight of the lighted schoolhouse caused flutters in my stomach. It was always a thrill getting a box of three pencils with my name on them from the teacher.

— *Alice L. Soffa*

Christmas programs were big events. I always had a piano or an organ. In one of my last schools, I taught piano and accordion at noon. I had an eight-piece accordion band, which made programs easy. At the end of one school year, I was given a TV table and lamp at the picnic as thanks for the music lessons.

— *Emily Sedlacek*

Christmas programs were always necessary, and we had to get all the children to participate. We had no musical instruments the first years, so the singing was not always kept in tune! Later, we got a phonograph, which helped a lot.

— *Signe Haraldson*

A Merrie Prairie Christmas

Christmas programs were a necessity. They were fun to have, with the makeshift curtains (sheets strung on a wire). My sister (also a teacher) and I bought a record player for the music. I had my program first. The record player was stolen before her program, so I had to sing behind the curtain to help her pupils out!

— *Eldora Nannestad*

School holidays were listed on the contract, as was the need to have Christmas programs. There were corn picking and seeding vacations, so we really managed only eight months of school.

For the Christmas program, a stage was set up with blocks, and planks were laid across them. Some schools had old curtains. If not, sheets were used. They sagged, wires broke, and down came the curtains! A placard with instructions was fastened with rope, so all the pupils had to do was walk on, follow the directions, and walk off. Children drew names and gifts were exchanged. Teachers gave a gift to each child and received one in return. Apples, which were furnished by the school board, were passed out to the audience. Teachers filled the children's sacks with goodies.

— *Arlie M. Klimes*

We enjoyed getting ready for programs for our parents. There were songs, recitations, and dialogues. We would practice and practice. Sometimes my brother, two sisters, and I could go through the whole program at home because we had learned everyone's part. Sometimes some of us were asked to put on a dialogue at a Farm Bureau meeting.

We always had a Christmas program for our parents. We had a big Christmas tree, on which we put real candles. We lit the candles on the night of our program when the schoolroom was packed with people. As I remember those Christmas trees, I still shake my head and wonder how we dared to do such a thing. We were so lucky.

— *Selma Anderson Hughes*

Christmas programs were big events for the whole neighborhood. The teacher would hang up sheets on wire for a curtain. We were all so excited. Of course there was no electricity, so lamps and lanterns had to be brought from the homes for this occasion. I especially remember one time when I was an angel and my wings kept falling off. I almost missed my cue for my part in the program!

We also had pie socials sometimes, where the men would bid on the ladies' pies. Entertainment was cheap in those days, and more things were done on the local level such as card parties and even dances in the farm homes.

— *Mary D. Thompson*

In December we worked hard getting a Christmas program together that we could present to the parents. I always enjoyed that when I was a child attending the country school. The school board erected a stage in the front of the building. After the program, there was a box lunch auction. The women of the district decorated a shoe box which contained lunch for two people. The men were good bidders and wanted to buy their spouse's box. If anyone knew which box was the teacher's, the bidding would usually go high, since the bachelors always wanted to get the teacher's box.

— *Agnes Brenden*

School holidays were memorable, as in the fall around Halloween or Thanksgiving, we would put on a program for the neighborhood, with singing, plays, pageants, recitations, etc. Following the program, the ladies' baskets, which had been decorated and filled with lunch, would be auctioned off to the highest bidder; then they ate the lunch together. This was great fun and exciting, especially if there were unmarried ladies in the group. Sometimes the bidding would really be competitive for these baskets.

The money from these auctions would then be used to buy Christmas gifts for the school children at Christmas time. The teacher bought these gifts, sometimes with the help of the parents. Some of the money was used to buy Christmas candy and peanuts, and also a box of apples. The candy and peanuts were then put in individual sacks and each child received one. The apples were passed out to everyone.

The Christmas program was quite an event. The real "Christmas Story" was always given as a pageant, along with much singing, other plays, and recitations. Someone always came in dressed as Santa Claus and distributed the gifts.

— *Margaret Thompson Cimenski*

Bonnie Hughes Falk: "Programs, Socials and Other Diversions," reprinted with permission from *Country School Memories*. Published by BHF Memories Unlimited, 1986. Distributed by Adventure Publications.

A Merrie Prairie Christmas

Christmas on the South Dakota Prairie

Shirley Holmes Cochell

The morning of December twenty-third, I set out for home across the snow-covered prairie on Eagle Chief, the bay gelding I rode when going after cattle for Mr. Saunders. He was a good horse but the years of twisting, turning, sudden stopping, and reversing as a stock horse had taken their toll. Eagle Chief's spavined legs, stiffened further by the cold, caused him to limp at first; but once we were on the road he was again his old self, mincing his way down icy slopes, avoiding drifts. He knew the prairie so well I turned him toward home and gave him his head.

Because of a late start and the slow travel, I arrived at noon and found the family at dinner in the kitchen.

Greeting me, Pa noted, "You've grown, filled out."

Serving my plate of boiled beef and vegetables, Ma expressed anxiety that the food might not be so good as the kind I had been accustomed to. I quickly reassured her that after my morning rides no other meal could be better.

Agnes, saying nothing, looked at me with wonder throughout the meal as though I were a stranger.

The Christmas season had brought the usual abundance of mail from relatives. It was read with even greater delight because this year we were so very far away from all of them. A letter from Aunt Mary, Ma's older sister who with Uncle Theis and their children lived on a prosperous farm near Plainview, Nebraska, recalled the grand vacation we had spent there one summer. She enclosed the usual picture of the farm and their ever-increasing herd of cows. Aunt Rose, whose farm in Minnesota we had also visited, wrote that she, Uncle Will, and cousins Florence and Joe planned to move to Texas. Plattsmouth postmarks indicated letters from Grandpa and from Uncle Pete who, with his family, lived on a farm adjoining Grandpa's, the old homestead where Ma was born.

Uncle Nick, the prosperous owner of the flour mill in Weeping Water, Nebraska, for whom Pa had been the Omaha agent, expressed interest in our progress in South Dakota and included news of Aunt Anna's social activities, cousin Mary's new interest in dramatics and accomplishments in violin and piano, and cousin George's athletic ability on high school football and baseball teams.

Uncle George, the "sourdough" whom we remembered so well for stories of his adventures in the Yukon, and Aunt Tinie were in California where he was trying, with little success, to sell Ford autos.

Uncle Joe, youngest of the Holmes family, had recently married and moved onto a farm in Arkansas.

Pa had received the wishes of "Froelich Weinachten" from his brother and many nieces and nephews in Germany. Some had sent photographs; but their letters, in German script, caused Pa some difficulty in translating.

Nick, who wrote a beautiful Spencerian hand, corresponded with Della Waters, a second cousin whom we had never met, in St. Helena, California. He had written one of his usual long letters and received an equally interesting one from her with glowing accounts of California, the Napa Valley in particular, and a set of pictures: the Old Bale Mill, the Stone Bridge, grape vineyards and fruit orchards, wooded scenes along the highway, the geysers, and Mt. St. Helena. A nostalgic letter for Agnes arrived from her Omaha chum Hermenia Leighleiter, expressing hope they might someday be together again.

Ed and Agnes were eager to talk about the Lyon Township Public School, a typical one-room schoolhouse, where their world centered around teacher, playmates, games, pictures, and books. They were delighted when Nick suggested we hitch a team to the sleigh and ride over there.

Near the humble building, the big snowman they had taken days to build stood guard, with battered hat, old scarf, pipe, and broom in hand. Leading us to the unlocked door, Ed quickly ushered us inside and eagerly announced, "All the decorations are being left until we return after vacation." Chains of colored paper festooned the room, and Christmas drawings covered the blackboard.

Teachers had come and gone to the little barbed-wire enclosed schoolhouse where grades were determined only by the "reader." With important work to be done on the farms, few scholars had reached the Eighth Reader, the accomplishment necessary to receive a diploma. Ed and Agnes praised their first teacher, a nineteen-year-old graduate of Carlisle Indian School in Pennsylvania: "He was fun and a good horseman — a real bronco buster!" Before the end of the term, he left and was followed by a niece of Mr. Balster, the school trustee whose family always boarded the teacher. A pleasant young woman with a deformed arm, she had probably accepted the post in order to complete her own grammar school education. She left to marry the young immigrant blacksmith in Gannvalley. Their current teacher was Miss Budlong, a buxom blonde from Minnesota who was enthusiastic about her first teaching position. In addition to seeing that the schoolroom was neat and clean, she had been responsible for an ingenious Nativity scene constructed with cutouts, cardboard, and watercolors. The scene was extended with colored chalk half the length of the blackboard, where far in the distance the three wise men were shown being guided by a silver star.

In answer to my question about attendance, Agnes said there were ten pupils, but added, "Most don't attend regularly."

Of the pupils, the one who had to travel the greatest distance was Carrie Clayton, a small pale girl of fourteen who rode an old sway-backed farm horse from her home which was south and across Smith Creek. Carrie had gotten lost in a blizzard the previous winter and caused much consternation until she was found. The two younger Burians to the west did not live a great distance but had to go around a wash and a coulee; the fact that only Bohemian was spoken in their home further hampered their learning. Ed and Agnes, a good mile and a half north of the school, seldom missed a day, perhaps as much for Pa's desire for "peace around the place," as for their education. The four Balster girls and their younger brother, to the east, were half of the class. School began when they and the teacher appeared in an old spring wagon; if the wind was right, their singing and shouts could be heard before they came over the rise.

Ed said he had heard attendance was better than ever this term and that classes had never been so large before. Even the older Burian boys Frank and Antone, as well as Gus and Tador Runge, had decided to brush up on their studies. It was reported that Miss Budlong, however, "being true to a young man back home," had refused all dates.

Early the next morning Ed and I rode horseback to Vega for a few purchases and mail. Ma was planning a Christmas dinner and had given us a list of items needed. There had been more snow during the night. We avoided the drifts and the snow-covered roads and kept to windblown higher ridges where we could. Ed's Prince, a small husky dog of mixed breed, followed closely behind.

It was still early when we got to Vega. The town was deserted except for one sleigh and team at the hitching pole in front of Fousek's store. A shotgun leaned against the seat, and a large freshly killed rabbit lay on an old blanket.

"Wonder whose sleigh that is?" asked Ed, as we dismounted. Peering through a clear place in the frost-covered window before we entered the store, he answered his own question. "It's 'Big' Sobek's. He's the oldest Sobek, and one *tough guy*!"

Inside the store, Big was hacking open a case of chewing tobacco. Although he was not a tall man, he did look big in his sheepskin-lined coat. He was a broad person with an inch or more of black beard, and he seemed even bigger because of his loud voice that could be heard all over. Ed said Big lived somewhere beyond the Crow reservation and that in spite of reports he had a wife and bunch of kids Ed didn't know anyone who had met them. His reputation included a mean disposition that had reportedly caused him trouble.

As we passed, there was no greeting, for Big was one of the characters if you don't greet first, "t'hell with you."

Quiet, meek Mrs. Fousek waited on us. We bought oranges, apples, some hard Christmas candies — a round kind cut from brightly colored sticks with flowers and other small designs in the white centers, and a striped variety fluted, twisted, and pleated — and some peppermints, Pa's favorite. Mrs. Fousek gave Ed one of the large wooden pails that the candy came in, noting there were a lot of crumbs still stuck in the bottom. Ed filled it with our purchases and hung it at the side of his saddle.

Upon arriving home, we realized Prince was nowhere in sight. As an hour or more passed we wondered what could have happened to him, for he had never strayed before. We finally saw him coming slowly over the rise in the road, stopping to rest occasionally. Forager that he was, we knew he had to be dragging something. With his rest periods becoming more frequent we went out to meet him and found, to our dismay, that Prince was dragging a rabbit almost as large as himself.

"Big's rabbit!" Ed exclaimed, knowing Prince had never been able to catch one. Could he possibly have dragged Big's rabbit out of the sleigh and all that distance?

Ed was terrified. "Big's a tough guy. He'll kill us if he thinks we stole his rabbit. There'll be a trail in the snow — blood spots and dragging marks. I expect we'll see his sleigh any minute. Big'll storm in here with fire in his eyes, teeth showing through that beard — he won't give us a chance to explain."

We could do nothing but wait. The rabbit remained in plain sight; hiding it would have been useless. As the long minutes passed, no horses, no sleigh, and no Big appeared. Ed finally stopped looking down the road. "Do you think he's accused someone else?"

I shrugged my shoulders. We often wondered, but never heard.

Jimmy Havlik had heard I was coming home and dropped in around noon to invite Nick and me to the Bohemian's Christmas Eve party that night at the hall above his uncle's store in Vega. It was more or less a family affair, a party of such gaiety that only the Bohemians could put on. The evening began with a Christmas Nativity play, staged by the children in appropriate costumes, after which they each stood in line to receive an orange, an apple, and a bag of candies. Games for the small children were directed by one of the teachers who had been invited, and everyone else danced to accordion music, continuous and in increasing tempo. How they danced, on and on, round and round: folk dances, square dances, the schottische and polkas!

Mrs. Havlik, Jimmy's mother, who had boasted of having had "fifteen children, seven living, all without benefit of doctor or midwife," and who always complained of her ills and told of her gall bladder operation at the Mayo Clinic in Rochester, Minnesota, entered the polka contest. Urged and cheered by friends, the contestants danced on and on. The accordion player showed signs of tiring, and one couple after another dropped out until only Mrs. Havlik and her partner Joe Urban, a strong young man, remained. Spinning around in the middle of the floor, they became the center of attraction. Enjoying the attention, they continued, encouraged by friends and disregarding some pleas to stop. At last, one of the older men placed his arms around the accordion player, forcing him to stop the music. Mrs. Havlik stood glassy-eyed, too dizzy to walk, and had to be helped from the floor.

"Why did you stop us?" she complained indignantly, feeling heroic perhaps, knowing she had won with a great show.

The party was lively, and the generally shy Bohemian girls were friendly and good mixers, probably because they felt at ease with their own group and since most of the families were related. The pretty girls were neatly, if not modishly, attired in dresses they had made themselves. Their hands, however, were rough and coarse, for they worked in the fields along with the men. Almost without exception, the girls and their sturdy, equally handsome brothers were good dancers.

Rosie Kovanda, one of the less popular girls and quite naive, seemed extremely happy, for some of the boys arranged a mock fight over her. They went outside to have it out and came back with clothes disarranged and faces smudged. She and many others thought it was real; those of us who knew would *never* give it away. By the time the evening ended, we had danced at least briefly with all the girls: Jimmy Havik's sisters Mary, Annie, and Stacey; the two Fousek girls Emma and Fannie; Mary Plos, Emma Burian, Annie Pitsek, Katie Simek, Lydia Jika, and a number of others. Nick enjoyed himself more than usual, particularly because he seldom went anywhere when I was not home.

A late supper was the final festivity. Coffee, made in a large blue enameled pot on top of the potbellied stove, was served with rich cream and sugar. The Bohemians apparently liked lots of cream. Along with pies and cakes, there were more kolaches (a Bohemian pastry) than one could eat. The happy, gay atmosphere continued as folks bundled up their sleepy children and headed home.

The next day was Christmas, different from the ones we had enjoyed in Omaha. Months of country living had made us all hearty eaters, and we insisted on big country style meals with lots of cream gravy, root vegetables such as parsnips and rutabagas, home-canned corn, tomatoes, homemade pickles, and mince and pumpkin pies. Winter was the season for an abundance of fresh pork and beef;

we did our own butchering and had it at its cheapest and best. Ma made sausages, head cheese, blutwurst, knockwurst, sauerkraut — all the German dishes she had been raised on. She pickled cucumbers and watermelon rind and made piccalilli. We had plenty of all the things we could grow. Ma added cranberries and assorted nuts from the general store and put together one of the best Christmas dinners to be had anywhere.

In the evening Nick and I got out the sled, hitched up the team, and drove toward Lyonville to see the Balster family, where the chief attraction was the four pretty girls. Mr. Balster very kindly greeted us and quickly disappeared. He was a good man who usually avoided people, perhaps because of a sensitivity about his appearance. His nose, chin, and one thumb had been shot off when his young son accidentally pulled the trigger of a shotgun the father was holding. A heavy black beard hid some of the scars.

The Balsters' large home reflected both refinement and femininity. Nora, about eighteen, and Alberta, near sixteen, both played the piano well and entertained us with music, stereoscopic slides, games, and delicious food including a variety of homemade candies and Christmas cookies. I also got to meet Miss Budlong, the school teacher, who had been accepted as one of the Balster family; she was everything Ed had said: vivacious, witty, and attractive.

The Balstar girls had the verve and glow of abundant good health and the beauty of rustic simplicity. Their voices were soft, and their manner easy and gentle. Though they were good company and nice to be with, both were almost too proper to be interesting as sweethearts but, no doubts, would make good mates someday for any man wanting a perfect farm wife.

After an enjoyable evening, Nick and I went to get our team and sled and found to our dismay they were gone. We could not even guess which direction Dick, the habitual runaway, would have headed.

Rather than let our fair hostesses know of our carelessness in not fastening our horses properly, we struck out for home on foot. Our light shoes and good clothes were scarcely the type one would choose for a winter hike through the snow. The two-mile walk afforded ample opportunity to consider the eruption this episode would cause at home.

When we arrived, the packed snow showed no trace of the horses' return. Before starting for the house I decided, in spite of cold wet feet, to look around. Luckily, in spite of the dark, I saw a shadow. The horses were standing with sled intact wedged between a hay-stack and a shed some distance from the barn. Our "merry Christmas," if not ruined, would certainly have been badly marred had it been necessary to report to Pa the loss of team and sled!

The following day, before I left to return to the Saunders ranch, Ma served the rabbit. She had marinated it with a little vinegar and a touch of spices. Of all the special foods Ma ever cooked, her rabbit, hunter style, was the best. Ed, however, still fearing that Big Sobek would get him, had little appetite.

Shirley Holmes Cochell: "Prairie Christmas." From *Land of the Coyote*, Iowa State University Press, 1972.

Mittens

Kevin FitzPatrick

When winter shivers me
like a swimmer dippling
into an icy pool
and though I'm wearing gloves
each finger stiffens
like a body in a long drawer,
I switch to mittens,
sheltering my fingers
like snowed-in friends
who thaw,
accept their close lodging,
and now and then
perform short skits
until the weather warms.

Kevin FitzPatrick: "Mittens." From *Blossoms & Blizzards*. Pegasus Prose, 1988.

Early North Dakota Christmases

H. Ted Upgren, Jr.

Christmas is surely a most important day in the life of American families. Yet for all its presumed fundamentality throughout the world — as American as apple pie and Chevrolet — we may be surprised to learn that the celebration of Christmas as we practice it today is a comparatively modern custom.

Who would have ever guessed that at the time of this nation's Declaration of Independence 200 years ago, December 25 was hardly recognized any differently than any of the other 364.

Religious leaders of our Pilgrim and Puritan ancestors, ironically, opposed recognizing Christmas as a religious or secular holiday. Massachusetts Puritans passed a law in 1659 making it illegal for anyone to stop their normal work and particpate in church services.

They may have been prompted to this by a move several years earlier by their European counterpart that outlawed religious services on Christmas and Easter. Church opposition to the celebration of Christmas lasted many years, in some parts of the coutry as late as 1855. If there was a celebration, Santa Claus, Christmas trees and gift giving were not too much a part of it.

Gradually religious opposition to the secular celebration of Christmas died out, and soon after the Civil War (1860s and 1870s) Americans began the celebration of Christmas with a set of customs borrowed from other countries and cultures, mixed them together and came up with a refreshing observance — young and spirited — of the coming of the Messiah, Promise of the World, shared by young and old alike.

In the following paragraphs we're going to take a look at some of North Dakota's earlier Christmases, and at some of the people that found themselves living on our wintry prairie on this universal holiday. Some celebrations perhaps were limited by the original Puritan ethic. Others were limited by hardship, but a few adopted Christmas merriment much like North Dakotans would decades later.

The first white man to visit what was to become North Dakota and leave some record of his being here during the Christmas season was Pierre Verendrye. On December 13, 1738, this man and his party began their homeward march to Portage LaPrairie from a Mandan Indian village on the Missouri River. On December 24 they arrived at an Assiniboin Indian village. Sometime before departure and/or enroute Verendrye became ill and perhaps for this reason no mention

A Merrie Prairie Christmas

is made of Christmas. It is surmised that the hardships of this journey precluded all thought of celebrating the day in any way.

About 60 years later a geographer and explorer by the name of David Thompson, enroute to the Indian villages on the Knife River, made the area around Dogden Butte (near Butte, N.D.) his Christmas camp. The year was 1797. Apparently, a telescopic view of the route ahead revealed a party of Sioux Indians waiting in ambush for travelers. Thompson's party concealed themselves in a sheltered area near the butte where they probably spent a very nervous Christmas Day. At 7 p.m. on that day Thompson recorded the temperature of 15 degrees below zero, certainly another factor that took the warmth out of this normally cheery day.

On Thursday, December 25th in the year 1800, Alexander Henry, a partner in the Northwest Company, an outfit that operated fur trading posts in North Dakota and other points in the Northwest, spent what appeared to be a relatively pleasant Christmas Day at one of his posts either near the mouth of the Park River in Walsh County or at the mouth of the Pembina River. An entry in Henry's journal reads, "Treated my people with high wine, flour and sugar."

Probably the most significant exploratory expedition ever to cross North Dakota occurred in 1804 and 1805 when Lewis and Clark spent the winter at Fort Mandan about 14 miles west of Washburn. They arrived at the Mandan village a bit in advance of the severe winter weather and therefore were able to prepare adequate winter shelters before the long winter set in. For this reason and because they had successfully completed the first leg of a dangerous journey, they had ample reason to celebrate Christmas Day of 1804. An account from the Biddle text of the Lewis and Clark journal reads:

"Tuesday, 25th, we were awakened before day by a discharge of three platoons from the party. We had told the Indians not to visit us as it was one one of our great medicine days; so that the men remained at home and amused themselves in various ways, particulary with dancing in which they take great pleasure. The American flag was hoisted for the first time in the fort; the best provisions we had were brought out, and this, with a little brandy, enabled them to pass the day in great festivity."

Maximilian, Prince of Wied, who became a well-known naturalist and scientist, left good records of his travels on the Upper Missouri. On Christmas Day in 1833 at Fort Clark, also in the Washburn area, he described festivities as follows:

"At midnight the engagés of the fort fired a volley to welcome Christmas Day, which was repeated in the morning; the 25th of December was a day of bustle in the fort. Mr Kipp had given the engagés an allowance of better provisions, and they were extremely noisy in their Canadian jargon. The poor fellows had no meat for some time, and had lived on maize, boiled in water, without any fat."

On December 25, 1834, Francois A. Chardon, an American Fur Company clerk stationed at Fort Clark, related in his journal the celebration of that Christmas Day:

"Thursday 25 Christmas comes but once a year, and when it comes it brings good cheer. But not here! As everything seems the same, No New Faces, No News, and worse of all No Cattle (buffalo), last Night at one half past ten O'clock we partook of a fine supper prepared by Old Charboneau, consisting of Meat Pies, bread, fricassied pheasants (probably sharp-tailed grouse), Boiled tongues, roast beef — and coffee — the brilliant assembly consisted of Indian Half Breeds, Canadians, Squaws and children, to have taken a Birds eyes view, of the whole group, seated at the festive board, would of astonished any, but those who are accustomed to such sights, to see in what little time, the Contents of the table was dispatched, some as much as seven to nine cups of coffee, and the rest in like proportion, good luck for the Cooks that they were of the Number seated at the table, or their share would of been scant as everyone has done Honour his plate...."

An unusual frontier character, Henry A. Boller, a member of the fur trading company at Fort Atkinson on the Missouri River which operated in opposition to the Fort Berthold trading post, apparently enjoyed frontier life and developed a sympathetic attitude towards the Plains Indians. His contentment on the prairie must have also permitted him to keep detailed journals. He makes the following comments about Christmas Day, 1858:

"A splendid day. Old Jeff says it is the pleasantest and finest weather he has ever experienced on the 25th ... Everybody dressed themselves in their best; I put on a new pair of pants, a red plaid flannel shirt, black silk cravat, and coat. It seemed odd to be dressed up so much after being so long accustomed to a free and easy style. St. Nicholas did not desert us, up in these frozen N-Western regions. I gave Mr. McBride a bottle of old Brandy (would that it had been a dozen); and he gave me a most magnificently garnished bullet pouch and shoulder strap for a powder horn; the work of his squaw, Susanne; the finest thing of the kind I ever saw ... Jeff Smith came over about noon, and his eyes fairly twinkled when the Bourgeois gave him a horn. After talking awhile, we went over to Fort Berthold to dine and did ample justice to the delicious prairie chicken and rabbit potpie, raisin puddings and pie; After a smoke, we returned, Jeff with us, to Ft. Atkinson, where our

A Merrie Prairie Christmas

Christmas Dinner was speedily set before us. It consisted of Mackerel, stewed oysters, sardines, bangs, molasses, coffee, and dried peach pie; the whole making a pretty fair spread ... After eating to repletion, we returned to our house ... the men from the Opposition had a regular frolic and stage-dance to the music of an accordion: they put on some squaws' leather dresses which I loaned them ... They kept going for several hours ... all deeply regretted the absence of any drinkables ... We read nearly all evening, but before I went to sleep, I thought of all the Christmases I had spent, and relived in my mind's eye the varied scenes in which I had been an actor, up to the present time and this, the first Christmas ever passed by me, away from the paternal roof."

"Cold — oh no — -31 this morning and -30 tonight and not above -15 all day.... "

This statement taken from Ferdinand A. Van Ostrands's diary indicates the frigid weather experienced on Christmas Day, 1871. A young man, Van Ostrand represented the last of the fur traders in North Dakota and helped pull the curtain on the end of the era. By the mid-1870s the large fur trading companies passed from the Dakota scene; the frontier had been conquered and settlement had begun. Some additional notes from Van Ostrand's diary from Christmas Day read:

"Christmas had been lively enough in some respects. Too much of the ardent circulating to allow things to pass off happily — we had a very good dinner — all things considered. Tappan and Mr. and Mrs. Bradford dined with us. The Major gave the Indians something to make their hearts good. Marsh and I gave the folks in the fort a little stuff."

The age of the explorer and trapper/fur trader had passed. Fargo was no longer the gateway to the frontier as Northern Pacific rails were laid west 200 miles to Bismarck. With the railroads came the infanry and cavalry to protect the builders of the iron horse road. Then, transported by this rapid conveyance, came the settlers. It began in the late 1860s and by 1900 over 30,000 family homesteads had been claimed across much of North Dakota. Of course, Christmases continued, despite hard times and this generally unprosperous settlement period.

Mrs. Kate Roberts Pelissier was a small girl and member of one such family whose head was a restless type that took homesteads near Mandan and Medora, the latter being close to Theodore Roosevelt's Maltese Cross ranch (south of Medora). In *Reminiscences of a Prairie Mother,* Mrs. Pelissier, living on her father's own place just south of the Maltese Cross, recalls the times were bad, but not so bad they went hungry; however, "there had to be 'cash money' too."

In her publication she states:

> "Uncle Howard Eaton sent Anne and me each a lovely doll with hair. [For her birthday earlier her two sisters made her a rag doll stuffed with river sand and from a buffalo forelock gave it long black hair.] He also sent a little doll for Nell, and books for the older girls. How happy we all were."

On another Christmas a hired man provided the Pelissier girls with the perfect present:

> "He let us choose from among three things that he would send away for. We picked out what we called a 'grind organ.' With it came about twenty 'rollers' for the pieces it would play. For holding these he fashioned a small cabinet, a pigeon-hole for each roller. To us children this hand organ was very wonderful and we spent many, many happy hours playing the records over and over."

In the fall of 1884, the John J. Robinson family arrived from St. Louis at the Bismarck railroad depot and made the 60-mile and three-day trip to their new log cabin near Coal Harbor (near what is now Riverdale). With the Christmas season advancing quickly it appeared there was little to offer for a merry Christmas. Young John Wade, currently a 98-year-old retired veterinarian and pharmacist living in Garrison, recalls in his publication, *Recollections*:

> " ... There were no evergreen trees native to this area ... however ... in exploring the area near the village we discovered that there was an abundance of evergreen 'creeping juniper' growing profusely along the high bluffs overlooking the Missouri River. This gave my oldest sister Mollie the incentive to improvise a Christmas tree ... she gathered a quantity of juniper and selecting a suitable small tree in the timber near the steamboat landing, she set up the tree in the front room and covered the branches of the tree by attaching the small strips of evergreen juniper to each twig ... With wild rose buds and thorn apples threaded in string the tree was decorated and with a few wax candles it made a real addition to Christmas. We had no oranges or apples that Christmas ... but Christmas morning we found our stocking well supplied with nuts, stick candy and old-fashioned gumdrops ... My greatest thrill was to wake up Christmas morning to find a bright shining saddle with real stirrups ... So this was my very first cow-boy outfit and it appeared with me in more than one early Fourth of July horse race."

The preceding accounts of early Christmases in Dakota remind us of the astonishing changes our Great Plains community has made in a relatively short time. The people who lived during these past periods were, by necessity, very close to the Dakota outdoors. In their holiday celebrations where merriment and joviality were earnestly embraced like these Christmases, the outdoors, its prairie, and its river bottomlands — from which came their requirements — controlled their festive moods.

Most late 20th century Christmases have been without privation. We are warm. Our fireplaces are cheerily aglow. Our tables are mostly level with gastronomic delights unheard of a century ago. We are clothed in synthetic get-ups designed mostly for looks and seemingly less for practicality. We are soft because of automobiles, motorboats, elevators and snowblowers.

More than ever we have reason to be thankful. More than ever we should remember the good news and the real meaning of Christmas.

H. Ted Upgren, Jr.: "Early North Dakota Christmases." Reprinted from *Across the Wheatgrass*, 1988. Available from Windfeather Press, Box 7397, Bismarck, ND 58502.

Christmas on the Ranch

Edgar R. "Frosty" Potter

Around the first part of December, us kids would start thinking that it wouldn't be long until Christmas. Out would come the Sears Roebuck catalog and, believe me, it would get a lot of going over during the next few days.

We would find just about every toy you could think of: iron fire engines, hook-and-ladder sets, mouth organs, wagons, wind-up toys, Jew's harps, skates, sleds, and most everything. Of course, our eyes were always larger than Pa's pocketbook but we always seemed to get a bought toy or two.

As there wasn't any real Christmas trees in our part of the country, we would have to settle for an Elm or a Box Elder or most any tree. To make the tree look green, we would tie pieces of moss on the branches and hang on strings of popcorn, cranberries and some chains made out of different colored paper. A few little tallow candles were snapped on the branches and we had as nice a Christmas tree as one would want.

We always had a snow shovel and a couple pails of water handy in case the tree caught fire. Those little candles, setting on the dry branches, could easily start a fire and burn us out before we could say "scat."

Among other things ordered from the catalog, we always got a thirty-pound pail of cream candies. The candy was carefully divided into ten equal portions and it was then up to each of us to take care of his share.

We could find candy hid in most every part of the ranch: under beds, tucked into the sleeve of an old sheepskin, out in the chicken house or wherever we thought no one could find it. The candy was a rare treat but we seemed to get more enjoyment out of using the pieces in place of matches to play poker. After a few nights of such use, the candy would look more like chocolate drops. Come time to eat them we didn't much care what color they were.

Twit and I slept in the attic with our bunk right alongside the heating stove chimney. A cracker box sat at the head of the bed with a kerosene lamp on it so that we could see to read after we had crawled in.

More than once we would fall asleep and leave the lamp burning all night. Whenever this happened we would catch the dickens from Pa who was afraid that we might accidently tip the lamp over and burn up the house.

We were always going to fix up a corner in the barn with a stove and some blankets. If the house did burn up during the winter, we would at least have a chance of reaching the barn and not all of us freeze to death. We never did get around to doing it and considered ourselves lucky that we never had a fire.

To help pass the long winter days and nights, we would lay in a good supply of books, particularly the five-cent paperback novels such as "Diamond Dick," "Young Wild West" and other blood and thunder stories. "Young Wild West" books were the favorite of us boys. They'd start out with "crack" or "bang-bang" and the hombre shot at would either bite the dust or high-tail it out of the country "muy pronto."

Young Wild West always had with him his girl friend, Ariette Murdock; his friends, Cheyenne Charley and wife, Anna; and Jim Dart and his sweetheart, Eloise Gardner. They always traveled around the country on horses. The Lord only knows where they slept and bought their grub.

Oh, yes! I near forgot the other two members of the outfit. They were a couple of Chinamen, Wing Wah and Hop Wah. Wing was the cook and Hop was a champion sleight-of-hand performer and practical joker.

They were all as gritty as sand and were always Johnnie-on-the-spot when there was trouble around.

Young Wild West used only a six-shooter and he could trim a fly's eyebrows at a quarter-mile with his shooting arm broke and one leg tied up. Cheyenne Charley was a buffalo-sharpsman and could lay a 550-grain lead slug dead center on an Indian's head at anything — up to and including three miles. The other partner, Jim Dart, always used a repeating Henry rifle. But I'm not about to tell you what he could do with it; you wouldn't believe me, no-how.

During the winter the only persons coming to visit would be the ranchers after their mail. Once in awhile they might bring their wives along and stay for a few games of cards or just sit and catch up on any news, if any.

One time we sure thought we hit the jackpot when Pa was up to Mandan and brought home an Edison phonograph. It sure was a dandy and the only one in the country. It used round cylinder records and had a big morning-glory horn that hung on a stand setting on the floor. I tell you, we could scarcely wait for the records to thaw out so we could play them.

We all soon had our favorites from "The Preacher and the Bear" to "Come Take a Skate With Me, Katie" to "Clancey's Wooden Wedding" and twenty or thirty others which gave us a wide choice.

We also had an attachment so that we could make our own records. As the records were made of wax, some kerosene on a rag would rub the little groves off so we could record anything we wanted. Of course, none of us could play the piano or sing worth a damn but we sure had fun razzing whoever tried it.

Edgar R. "Frosty" Potter: "Christmas on the Ranch." Reprinted with permission from *Whoa...Yuh Sonsabitches*. Griggs Printing & Publishing, 1977.

Ma's Christmas Tree

Bill Lowman

It's all a part of Christmas
fetchin' Ma's tree in the cold
I could have took ol' Wrangler
but he's gettin' kinda old

> So I caught up little Badger Gray
> and pulled down my old scotch hat
> When things ain't right around him
> he turns inside out, quick as a cat

My stomach was gettin' empty
It was almost dinner time
I had Gray rode down pretty good
We'd been through a mighty climb

> Over in the cedar breaks
> quite a ways from home
> The snow was crusted 'most knee high
> over the dusty loam

I was draggin' Ma's tree with a rope
when the rope went under his tail
He gathered all four and went to the sky
you could say we really set sail

> Every time we came back down
> his rump that axe handle would hit
> I'd better pull all the leather I can
> for danged sure he ain't gonna quit

Thought I was done for a couple of times
but managed to gather back in
You're just gonna have to forgive me, Lord
if cussin's considered a sin

> He paused for a second when he hit
> next to a creek bank trail
> It was then I saw my chance had come
> and jerked it free from his tail

We're both sweatin' and tremblin' now
and hurtin' bad from fatigue
I looked over my shoulder
Ma's tree ain't nothin' but a twig.

> Cowboy poet Bill Lowman: "Ma's Christmas Tree." From
> *Riders of the Leafy Spurge*. Bill Lowman, 1985.

Around
the
Christmas
Tree

Our First Christmas Tree

Russell Duncan

My father and I went to town one day shortly before Christmas with a load of grain. I heard my mother and father talking before we left for town. Mother told Dad to cut off a good-sized branch from a tree on our way home. Sure enough, on the way home, while I held the lines, Dad went into a clump of trees where he cut off a branch which he put in the sleigh. I had no idea what he wanted the branch for — I was puzzled but didn't say anything.

When we got home we went to do chores. When we came in to supper, my mother and the other children seemed especially happy. I wondered why they were so happy. They said, "Come into the front room." I went in, and there to my surprise was the branch we had brought home in the sleigh. It was all decorated with different colored crepe paper and pieces of cloth. To me it was beautiful. That was our first Christmas tree. I can remember it as well as though it were yesterday.

On Christmas morning when we got up we opened our gifts. We didn't each receive many presents — we really enjoyed what we did get. I got a big red apple and a Jack-in-the-Box that looked like a camera. The trick was to have someone look at the glass at the front of the box, on the pretense of taking their picture. While they were looking intently, you would press a button that would cause a paper snake about two feet long to jump out. I tried it on everyone, including my folks, several times. After the first two or three times my victims knew what to expect so it wasn't much fun.

I knew that my aunt and uncle were coming over for dinner. I just couldn't wait to play the trick on my aunt — take her picture. She posed very nicely, I pressed the button and out jumped the snake. It landed in her lap. It was a surprise to her so it scared her half to death. She made such a commotion that it frightened me too. However, I continued to "take pictures" until my camera wore out.

We children had no trouble deciding on a Christmas present for our mother that year. We had eaten loganberry sauce and just loved it. Commercially canned fruit was a luxury in those days so we decided that's what we would give our mother — a can of loganberry sauce.

We kept it hidden until Christmas although we often looked at it, admiring the tempting looking picture of the loganberries on the label.

At last Christmas came. Mother was so pleased with her gift. Although we had kept it hidden upstairs, Mother no doubt knew what we were looking at so often but really expressed surprise when she received it.

We urged her to open the can immediately — our mouths were really watering for a taste of the delicious berries. When she did open it, we shared it and enjoyed her gift as much as she did.

I even kept the empty can with the brightly colored label as a toy for a long time.

One year Mary and Grace received dolls for Christmas. I was fascinated by the dolls. They were very special to my sisters so they wouldn't let me touch them except under special conditions.

One of the neighbor children received a Teddy bear for Christmas. I thought this was really nice and wished I had one. Even though it was after Christmas, Dad said he would get me one. When he went to town the Teddy bears were all sold out so I didn't get one. Dad said they did have a black doll and asked if I would like that. I decided that would be fine.

Each day as Dad returned from town, from hauling grain, I waited for his return and my doll. Finally the big day came. Dad handed me a package. I dashed into the house and unwrapped it — sure enough here was my black doll. I was overjoyed. Mary and Grace both wanted to share in it and play with it. I think I did let them play with it occasionally but always kept a close watch on it.

It is surprising how a child becomes attached to a toy. I kept that doll for several years. In fact I gave it to my brother Merritt, when I got too old to play with dolls and he became old enough. By that time one arm was missing but he still liked it.

Russell Duncan: "Our First Christmas Tree." From *I Remember*, Russell Duncan, 1975.

A Merrie Prairie Christmas

The Glory Tree

Faye Cashatt Lewis

One teacher we had at Sunnyside was a charming woman who has remained linked in my mind inseparably with the Christmas celebration she arranged for us that year. I see her now as she stood before us beside her desk, a slender figure in a white shirtwaist and a black skirt that reached almost to her ankles, her hair a shiny, smooth cap with a coil on each side of her head, her face radiant with planned joys for her beloved pupils sitting expectantly in front of her.

She wore her watch half-way down the front of her shirtwaist, hung by a chain around her neck. The lid opened noiselessly when she pressed the stem, but it closed with an authoritative snap that could be heard all over the schoolroom. She seldom looked at her watch except at the close of a fifteen-minute class period, and she seemed to know when that was, before looking. It was just a part of the closing routine. In the same way that a modern school might use electric bells, the closing of Teacher's watch clicked forward another cog in the day's schedule.

But the watch made another sound sometimes — a soft, muted meshing of the thin gold lid, which was only faintly audible. I never could determine exactly what made this changed sound, but she seemed to be holding the watch cupped more closely, even lovingly, in her hand at these times. Perhaps we only imagined this change of sound, seeing in her pretty face the benign look of a contemplated happiness for a roomful of children. For just as the click signaled the end of a usual class period, this soft watch sound meant some pleasant variation in the day's routine.

Hearing it now, in this after-recess final quarter of the school day we awaited with alert expectancy whatever it was that Teacher had in mind. Pencils were laid down, papers stopped rustling, my seatmate closed her history book and put it back in the desk. Teacher corroborated our hopeful anticipation by standing quietly for a few moments, prolonging the delightful suspense. On ordinary days she would already be unrolling the map for seventh-grade geography class.

Coming, as this did, on Monday of the second week of December, we guessed that Teacher's plan had something to do with Christmas. Most things we did these days had Christmas woven into them. When Teacher would ask, "What shall we do for opening exercises this morning?" there would be a flurry of excitedly waving hands. And whichever child she called upon, his request was apt to be, "Let's talk about Christmas," or "Let's sing some Christmas songs."

We loved this, even we three older ones, who liked to consider ourselves past childish delights. Teacher loved it too, and this feeling of hers made warm and personal the stories of the Christ child, the wise men, Bethlehem, and the star. And the singing! — for the talking was always interspersed with a Christmas song or two. Our school had an organ, which many schools did not have, and when Teacher sat down and played "Silent Night" we felt rich with happiness and tingled with it as we sang.

Some of the talk would be about Christmas legends, family customs, and celebrations of the Holy Day in other lands. Teacher told us many stories her mother had told her about the old-time festivities in Sweden.

Customs that had to do with the Christmas tree held the younger children entranced. I could remember Christmas trees from my earlier childhood, before we came to Dakota: the still cold of the winter night, the crunching of snow under our feet as we walked to the church, the roomful of warmth, and the excitement inside. In the front of the church, at one side of the pulpit, would be the tall tree, aglitter with gifts and decorations and the flicker of candles, the latter watched over with some trepidation by our elders.

I had seen all this and remembered it vividly, but most of the younger children in this prairie had no recollection of a really full-grown tree of any kind, and a gaudily decorated one could exist for them only as a fantasy. One morning Teacher had varied our Christmas talk by letting each child say what he wished most as a gift, and a quite a number of them had chosen a Christmas tree.

Just a few months ago Mrs. Harkness had made a trip back to Pennsylvania to her mother's funeral, taking her little daughter Ann with her. At Ann's first sight of some trees out the train window she had cried out in amazement, "O Mama! Look at the big plants!"

I had heard this story repeated among the grown-ups several times, and it was always greeted with laughter. But it was a homesick-ish kind of laughter, never very boisterous.

Now when Teacher made her looked-for announcement that we would have no more lessons today, and that we should put our school things away, she waited until the crackle of papers, the rattle of slates and slate pencils, and the thud of books being thrust forcibly into desks, had subsided. Then she took a clean eraser and smoothed off every trace of chalk from the middle section of the blackboard. Next, with twenty-three pairs of eyes watching intently, she lifted the lid of her own desk and took out boxes of colored chalk.

"Children," she said, "instead of talking about Christmas trees this afternoon, suppose we make one for ourselves, here on the blackboard. Would you like that?"

It was a rhetorical question, answered by an ecstatic chorus of sighing, indrawn breaths. She took up a brown crayon first, and made a few vertical lines in the middle of the lower half of the blackboard.

"We could make the trunk black," she said, "but that wouldn't show so well on the blackboard. So we will use brown. Now how about the rest of the tree? What color shall we make it?"

A half-dozen pairs of small hands waved in the air.

"Green!" several of the children said, but there was a liberal sprinkling of "Purple!" "Red!" "Blue!" choices.

"Oh, children," Teacher said, "didn't we read that Christmas trees are evergreens? So wouldn't green be a better choice for our tree here?"

There was a preponderance of emphatic nods and yeses — but looks of disappointment, notwithstanding, on the faces of the proponents of reds, blues, and purples.

And then, although none of us thought of it as anything unusual at the time, Teacher demonstrated that she had the soul of an artist. what matter if trees look green to everyone else? Who knows the color of joy in the eyes of a child?"

"It's your tree," she said gently. "We'll make it any color you choose."

Nimbly her fingers manipulated the crayons, using the colors at the children's dictation. First, the network of major branches, then smaller and smaller ones, and finally the twigs. The result was a more pleasing harmony than anyone could imagine, seeing it described dully in print. It was like a green tapestry, with bits of the rainbow glowing through it. Or can it be that it is only a trick of my memory — preserving it thus?

As the tree took shape, the children added further decorations out of their own fancies. The little Lebert girl, a usually shy fifth grader, started it by exclaiming, "That red she is putting on now is a hair ribbon for me!"

Most of the other children took up the game, and Teacher let them talk, turning only to give them a brief admonitory look when they became too boisterous.

"I see my Christmas doll!"

"My drum is clear on top!"

"That's my train, winding 'round and 'round!"

Even my seatmate and I, big girls that we were, could imagine scarfs and handkerchiefs in a maze of colors.

When it was finished, Teacher wiped the chalk off her fingers with a dust cloth, and turned to the room with a glowing face.

"So we'll really have a tree of our own this Christmas, won't we? " she said.

One of the Purdy twins raised his hand. "Where will we put it?" he asked.

In an instant the fragile illusion was shattered. There was no longer a gift-laden tree in the room. The thing on the blackboard was only another picture like the ones in books.

It was a few moments before the dismay in Teacher's face could be marshaled into something constructive, something with which to meet this crisis. It was a dismay in which impatience or irritation had no part. Only disappointment, modified by pity, that here was one child who had not been able to lose himself with the rest of us in the delights of make-believe.

Meanwhile, like a cloud in the air, there was a question awaiting an answer.

By the time she gave it, Teacher's face had regained its composure. With a deliberate slowness that gave emphasis to her words, she told him, "We'll put it right here beside my desk where everyone can see it best."

It was no lightly spoken reply. The hush in the room testified to the solemnity of the moment, as of a vow being spoken, or a name being signed to a momentous paragraph.

The rest of us were completely mystified. Teacher and the Purdy twin were the only ones with any understanding — his on faith, hers on some kind of inner determination that we were unable to fathom.

Then she proceeded to mystify us still further. "We'll have Program Friday this week, too," she said. "Be sure to ask your parents all to come if they can."

Program Friday just before Christmas, when we were only now learning our pieces for the Christmas program? When would we get ready for it? Besides, we had had Program Friday only last week. We usually had it only once a month.

Teacher calmly went on to explain. "We won't learn anything new for this program. We'll use some of the songs and the poems we have had during the year. And don't forget to tell your fathers and mothers we'd like them all to come."

That was some Program Friday? It was the shortest one we had ever had. Just a couple of recitations, and a story the sixth grade had had for a language lesson. Then we all sang "Flow Gently Sweet Afton," and were dismissed.

Teacher told the smaller children they might play quietly for awhile in the back of the room, while she talked to the parents around her desk. We three older ones were assigned to the evening school chores.

The boy brought in the coal and kindling for Monday morning's fire, while the other girl and I cleaned the blackboards, dusted erasers, and tidied up in general. Most of the jobs we two did kept us not far from Teacher's desk, so we could hear most of what was said.

"I have promised the children a Christmas tree this year," Teacher told the group of parents.

Everybody looked amazed, and for a time no one said a word. They all knew, almost to a tree, the only evergreens for miles around. They were the ones on the Carlson and the Evans places. Most of the other settlers had planted some, too, but they had not survived. They all knew, too, the constant tending that had kept these few extant. In the hot summer, during the long July and August drought, when all the wells were low and some of them dry, Sadie Carlson had watered their trees as faithfully as she had their cattle. Pulling up water hand over hand with rope and pail from the stock well near the barn, she had carried it to the thirsting trees every evening after the sun was off them, and was now rewarded by the blessed fact that they were still alive and getting their moisture more easily from winter snows. The Evans trees were a second planting, as their first ones had all died — three rows of little pines, most of them less than three feet tall, set hopefully along the north side of the building lot as a future windbreak.

Cut one of these trees down? It was too unthinkable a suggestion to be put into words, even as a dubious question.

Teacher hastened to explain. "It was this tree I drew for them on the blackboard that gave me the idea," she said. "I know we couldn't have a pine tree, or any other kind of evergreen. But couldn't we find just an ordinary little tree, or even a bush, somewhere? I thought we could wrap the branches with colored paper. We wouldn't have to use up big pieces; just scraps would do. The children could help me do it, at recess times, so it wouldn't take time from their lessons. I think we could make it real pretty, and they would all love it, I know."

As Teacher tumbled out her words with such a pleading urgency to them, the shocked resistance among the group of parents weakened visibly. The director's wife unpursed her mouth, and the tenseness in most of the other faces relaxed.

"Well, I expect we could find some kind of little tree, couldn't we?" one of the women asked.

It was father who put the stamp of finality on the plan. "I've got that bunch of plum brush where Lute's Creek cuts through a corner of my pasture," he said. "We could cut a tree there. Fact is, they could do with a little thinning out."

Other suggestions followed. Quite a few plum trees grew along the Keya Paha River, and most of the settlers knew where there were a few choke cherry trees. Several women shook their heads at this latter suggestion. They needed the choke cherries for jelly ("even if they don't jell right," one woman interpolated); wild plums were more plentiful.

In the end it was decided to take father's offer, after he reiterated his statement that we could spare a tree from our thicket. It would be most of a day's trip to the nearest point on the Keya Paha, and the road went through numerous draws that were sure to be full of drifted snow. Better to depend on something nearby than to make a long trip at this time of year.

Mrs. Carlson offered a wooden bucket, painted green, that could be filled with sand to hold the tree. She had had geraniums planted in it, but in the first sudden cold snap of the winter she had forgotten to move it back from the window one night, and they had all frozen.

And now to the decorations. Interest had quickened to an excited buzzing of conversation, mostly among the women. There was no one among them who did not have something to contribute. Scraps of colored tissue paper left over from making May baskets or valentines or artificial flowers, ends of fancy shelf paper, carefully hoarded wrappings from a rare box of bon bons, the tinsel lining from packages of tea. One woman had a part of a roll of ceiling paper with silver stars dotted over it. The children could cut them out to make ornaments. Yards of popcorn could be strung, and wound in and out among the branches.

"If we only had some cranberries, like we had back east," one woman said, wistfully. "They make such pretty strings."

"I'd be in favor of eating them, if we had them," her husband countered.

In the fall the McElway girls had strung some of the red seed pods from wild rose bushes. They would be willing to lend them, their mother knew, if they could be put high on the tree out of the reach of the smaller children.

With plans once made, there was no dallying in carrying them out. Before Teacher rang her hand-bell for nine o'clock school on Monday morning the tree had been brought in and set in its bucket of sand. It was a drab and scraggly object, in actuality, but we looked at it in the light of what our faith in Teacher made of it, a promise of rare joy and beauty.

"When do fix it?" clamoring voices were asking, as we took our seats.

But Teacher was firm. "We'll practice our Christmas songs for opening exercises," she said, "and then to our lessons. Recess is the time for fixing the tree."

Teacher had to relax the strictness of this regime, however, after a few days' try at it. By the time she could get ready the pot of flour paste, and organize the children into cutting and pasting squads, there was not enough time left in a fifteen-minute recess period to do much of the actual decorating.

Recess periods were lengthened to half hours, and there were several longer after-school sessions before the job was finished. Teacher salved her conscience for thus curtailing lesson time by telling us sternly that there would have to be a lot of makeup work done right after Christmas.

But none of us worried about future penalties for today's enjoyment. No schoolroom, no beehive, ever presented a picture of more concentrated industry than our school did in these tree decorating sessions. We older ones did the cutting of the strips of paper, while the smaller children daubed the paste on ends, wiping their sticky fingers with abandon on shirt fronts, overalls, and little aprons. At first Teacher gave some concern to the protecting of small garments, but when she saw several of them licking their fingers instead, she decided to ignore the disposition of the surplus paste, restricting her supervision to the mechanics of the decorating job proper.

After the preparation of the strips of paper came the job of applying them to the tree. Teacher and the seventh-grade boy could both reach the very tip of the tree with sufficient ease, so the top flight artistry was allotted to them. Other areas were distributed on down in proportion to the varying heights of the children, and there was work for all. Even the smallest of them became adept at falling in with the work pattern — choose a branch or twig, and a strip of prepared paper estimated to be of the proper length to be wound around and around to cover the twig, with enough lap-over to paste down the end securely.

Teacher countenanced a constant low-voiced chatter as we worked, but she promptly quelled any show of boisterousness as not conducive to efficiency. It was apt to accompany torn strips, spilled paste, and even a tumble of one of the more daring little boys off the edge of Teacher's desk, where he had attempted to stand to lengthen the reach.

Occasionally Teacher would try to organize the talk with the same Christmas stories and legends we had been having during the school periods. But she found this inadvisable, too, for any prolonged time. She would be working away and at the same time retelling the story of Scrooge and Tiny Tim, or of Bethlehem and the wise men, and look up suddenly to see all hands idle, interest in the story having carried everyone completely away from the job at hand.

Little German Katy, in primary class, who could speak scarcely a word of English when she started to school in the fall, found all this talk about Christmas, "Glory to God in the Highest" and "Peace on Earth" too much for her newly sprouting vocabulary to encompass, and she began calling the tree "der glory Baum." When Teacher told the rest of us what it meant, a number of others took up the name in good-natured derision, and in not time at all our tree was universally referred to as "glory tree."

From time to time some of the parents dropped in to see how things were progressing, and from their mysterious, low-voiced conferences with Teacher, we gathered they were having some part in our Christmas Eve plans, too. Snatches of conversation I overheard while I was helping the twins with their wraps one evening — in a very dilatory manner, most likely — indicated there had been some discussion of gifts to be put on the tree for all the children alike. Teacher already had a gift for each child, she said.

Someone suggested oranges, but this idea received only fleeting consideration. It was not certain that oranges were obtainable in town, and if they were, who could think of buying twenty-three of them all at once? More than that; there would have to be enough for the small children under school age who would be coming to the program. Oranges were not a staple provision in any of our homes; they were always something special. At our house, for example, an orange was a traditional gift for father to bring home to a sick child who was on the mend and just beginning to have an appetite again.

While this discussion was going on an idea occurred to me, the voicing of which was almost painful to suppress. There stood Mrs. Roberts, not saying a word. Every fall some relatives in Illinois sent the Robertses a barrel of apples from their orchard. And what a pleasure it was to go to the Roberts house in fall or winter on an errand! Any caller at their house was certain to be treated to an apple before he left, and usually several to take home with him for the rest of the family. Several times Mrs. Roberts had let me go with her to the vegetable cave to get a bowlful of them. Any other cave I had ever been in had the musty, sprouty smell of long-stored potatoes, cabbages, and turnips. In the Roberts' cave the only smell was the sweet, tangy one of the apples. The apples took over completely. Oh Mrs. Roberts, I prayed, please give use some apples for the tree!

Mrs. Roberts did not fail me. She was a quiet, dignified woman, and it was her custom to think things out well before speaking. She had married late in life and had no children of her own. She had been a Teacher before coming to Dakota, and she still had most of her old school books. My most frequent errand there had been to borrow some of these books to supplement my own texts. I could not understand it then, but when I asked to borrow one of these books after another, she seemed as pleased as though I were doing her a favor. Now, as she offered the apples for the tree she seemed to have the same attitude about them, as though the pleasurable benefits of the gift were accruing to her instead of us.

From the time the tree project was started I was aware that my mother had some plan of her own about gifts. She did not tell me what it was, at first, but as the time became shorter she needed my help with it in the evenings after the twins and the boys had gone to bed. She was making little baskets of cardboard and stiff paper, and decorating them with fringed tissue paper, tiny paper flowers, and other oddments of color. She made twenty-three of them, one for each pupil and then a larger, very special one, for Teacher.

What to put in them called for discussion. Popcorn was the only treat that was plentiful. Mother longed to make a big batch of fudge, enough to put a piece, or maybe two, in each basket, but Father vetoed this firmly. It would take a week's supply of sugar, and we could not afford that. None of the settlers could afford luxuries of any kind. The payments they were to make on their land within a few months were constantly in their minds, and this opportunity for a deed to land of their own must not be forfeited by careless extravagance. A suggestion that bags of candy might be bought to put on the tree for all the children had been vetoed just as firmly. None of the settlers felt that they could contribute to such an unnecessary expenditure. so Mother contented herself with a compromise filling for her Christmas baskets; each was heaped generously with popcorn and had a single piece of molasses taffy on top.

School holidays started the day before Christmas. That afternoon several of the mothers came to help Teacher with the final arrangements. None of the pupils was allowed to come, not even the older ones. The last rehearsal of songs, dialogues, and recitations had been held.

People began arriving at the schoolhouse shortly after seven that evening. Most of them came in bobsleds, but our family walked. Having only a half-mile to go, none of us questioned that it was better for us to walk that short distance, even facing the icy north wind as we had to do, than to have the horses standing out in the cold needlessly for several hours. It would be still colder going home but the wind would be at our backs.

We carried a lantern with us to help us avoid the deeper drifts, and to keep us from floundering about uselessly in the snow. A number of the other settlers had lanterns with them, too, and we used them for light inside the schoolhouse. There were enough to hang one in each corner of the room and one behind the tree, and to set one on Teacher's desk.

The little room was crowded. Heavy wraps were hung on the hooks along the rear wall until no more could be accommodated, then laid in piles on the floor, keeping the belongings of each family segregated, as far as possible, to avoid confusion in finding them again. People sat on the seats, on the floor, or stood along the walls. A few had brought their own chairs with them in the bobsleds. The only clear spot in the room was in the middle, around the red-hot stove that held sway like a half-frightening sun, keeping us all comfortable so long as we didn't get too close. The occasional odor of scorched wool or rubber, when someone was careless with his coat or overshoes, was a warning.

But the tree, the fabulous tree, was the center of attention. Hanging from its multicolored twigs and branches were the silver stars, the popcorn strings, Mother's little baskets, Mrs. Roberts's apples, and little booklets for all the pupils from Teacher. On it and under it were gifts parents had brought for their children: dolls, tops, and other toys, and a few gifts for the adults themselves. These gifts were usually not wrapped, the name being fastened somewhere on the gift itself, not to a beribboned box that held the contents a secret. In these gifts, beauty and sentiment were sometimes sacrificed to practicality. One man bought a washing machine wringer as a Christmas gift for his wife and put it under the tree for her. She said she had needed a new one badly, and appeared well pleased with the thoughtfulness of his selection. Her reaction seemed so genuine one wondered if she might not have scolded him if he had chosen something frivolous for her.

"How could we ever have had a Christmas celebration without a tree?" people asked one another. It was the background for all the performers on the program; looking at it helped to keep the little children quiet; it was the tangible symbol of Christmas joy for everybody.

Tension built up in the room as the program advanced toward the delightful climax of gift distributing. Nothing more was needed, one would have thought, but there was a surprise yet to come. Teacher's mother and father had come over from Gregory County to take her home with them. They arrived late, when the program was nearly over, and had done so with a purpose, it developed. With them was Teacher's grandfather who had come in the fall to make his home with his son. He had been a factory worker in Ohio before his retirement, and for years had been in demand at holiday time as Santa Claus for various business firms. He had brought his suit with him when he moved here to his son's home, and he wore it tonight.

It was almost more excitement than the little folks could stand to see the whiskery, red-suited figure, familiar to them in pictures, thus come to life in our midst. Some were too over-awed to move or make a sound; some laughed and clapped hysterically; several of them cried. His arrival and the subsequent distribution of gifts turned the remainder of the evening into a happy hubbub of talking and laughter, crunching of apples and popcorn, mix-ups of gifts and

A Merrie Prairie Christmas

wraps, looking for lost caps and overshoes, a piece of half-chewed taffy caught in one little girl's curly hair.

Before I went to bed that night I set my gifts out on the dresser that I shared with the twins. My booklet from Teacher had pansies on the cover and was tied with a lavender silk cord with tassels on the ends. The poem in it was Elizabeth Barrett Browning's "The Swan's Nest." It was in my Fifth Reader. I loved it, and knew it by heart, but this familiarity made the gift all the more pleasing, and the poignancy of the closing lines, "But she would never show him, never, The swan's nest among the reeds," still could bring me tears.

There was something I had to think out before I went to sleep, and it took me a long time. It had to do with my mother and Teacher, and Mrs. Roberts. This thinking was prompted by the little baskets Mother had made. In some way Mother was like these other two women — Mrs. Roberts with her book learning, and Teacher with her soft hands and pretty clothes, all of which attributes were so foreign to my mother. Yet in some way she belonged with them; I was certain of it.

After much tortured thinking I was able to define the common denominator of quality possessed by these three as a greater caring-ness for others. Not just her own five children filled my mother's heart. She was concerned for the happiness of them all, in the same way that Teacher and Mrs. Roberts were. Yes, these three, among all the women in the community, belonged in a group apart.

This was a wonderful discovery for an adolescent to come upon, and it was my most precious and lasting gift from the glory tree.

Faye Cashatt Lewis: "The Glory Tree." From *Nothing To Make a Shadow*. Iowa State University Press, 1971.

The Silver Ornaments

Frances Wold

Each year the battered box of little silver Christmas tree ornaments sets me to remembering that holiday season over 40 years ago. A few of the ornaments have been broken, and their silver luster has dimmed a bit, but they will hang on my tree this Christmas just as they have each year since they were new, back in the depression days of the 1930s. They are a reminder of a time and place that now exist only in memory.

I was eighteen years old and teaching my first term of country school. Winter had come early that year, and day after day the little schoolhouse perched high on a hill was raked by bitter winds that piled the snow deep under its eaves. The weather matched the mood of the parents of my twenty-four pupils; crop failures and continued hard times had brought them close to desperation. Many of the children lacked warm clothing, and their lunch pails often contained only bread and syrup sandwiches.

The approaching holidays only deepened the gloom, as it was clear there would be no money for gifts or "extras." "Maybe we shouldn't even bother with a program this year," a father said to me one morning when he brought his youngsters to school. "Nobody's in much of a holiday mood anyway!"

However, this idea produced such an uproar among the children that he hastily withdrew his suggestion.

The children and I planned a program of recitations, songs and dialogues, ending with a nativity scene. They practiced faithfully, coaching one another until they were letter perfect in their parts.

They festooned the room with what seemed like miles of chains made from red and green construction paper. They fashioned crepe paper bows to cover the ugly cracks in the plaster walls. They colored pictures of fireplaces with stockings hanging from the mantel (though most of them had never seen a fireplace) and of Santa and his sleigh, and tacked them to the molding that encircled the room.

As the great day approached they drew names for gifts, with the limit for each set at ten cents. I put my name in the drawing also, as I did not want them to feel obligated to buy "Teacher" a special gift.

The excitement was evidently contagious at home, for one mother wrote a note saying that she would bring decorated cookies for everyone, and another volunteered to make popcorn balls. Welcome as these offers were, I still worried about "treats" for the children. Out of my small pay check I had to pay board and room, and there was not much left when I had bought a few other necessities. However, I determined that there would at least be a box of Crackerjack for each child.

Then one evening two of the fathers lingered in the schoolroom after the children had left. "We've decided it wouldn't be right if the kids didn't have some nuts and candy," one of them said, "so each family is going to put in a dollar to buy treats. We'll get them ready, so you won't have to worry about it."

"Times may be hard," the other added, "but after all, it's Christmas."

The weekend before the program I went to town in a bobsled with the family where I boarded, and bought a Christmas tree. It was on the skinny side, and it listed sharply at the top, but the storekeeper let me have it for 25 cents. At the last minute I gave in to temptation and bought the box of silver ornaments that looked so lovely in their tissue-paper nests.

The children loved the tree, crooked though it was, and they eagerly set to work to trim it. They strung the popcorn I had bought, and made more paper chains. They covered walnuts with tinfoil from the inside of cigarette packages, and made a cardboard star for the tip-top branch and covered it with more of the foil. As the finishing touch, we hung the little silver ornaments. I wished for lights, but we had none. The children thought it was beautiful just as it was.

The day before the program the youngsters brought their gifts for each other and piled them under the tree, along with the letter holders they had made for their parents from paper plates sewed together with colored string. By now the children were so excited that the room fairly crackled with anticipation

That same day one of the men arrived with planks and nail kegs to build a stage, something we had not thought of. "If you're going to do something, you might as well do it right," he said. He also set more planks and kegs at the back of the room for extra seating.

We used a sheet to curtain off a corner to serve as a dressing room, and, after a dress rehearsal on our new stage, we were ready at last.

The weatherman was on our side, for the night of the program was cold, but clear and still. By 7:30, every family had arrived, and were joined by others from the community. For once the tin-jacketed stove, stoked with lignite, warmed the room without smoking, and the gasoline lamps brought from my boarding place cast a white light over the proceedings.

There were few new clothes in evidence, but bright hair ribbons, stiffly starched shirts and freshly polished shoes made the children look very festive, indeed. Their elders were no less festive, all in their somewhat threadbare best, and plainly determined for this one night, at least, to forget the cares that weighed so heavily. All of them extravagantly admired the room decorations and the tree, to the children's great satisfaction.

The children performed nobly, even if a few voices trembled from stage fright, and though a little first-grader backed off the stage, hurting only his dignity. A small Joseph and a still smaller Mary gazed solemnly at the straw-filled manger, and subdued shepherds knelt as two eighth-grade girls in white crepe paper costumes sweetly sang "It Came Upon the Midnight Clear."

The program ended to great applause, and then a woman called out, "Teacher, we have a surprise for you!" One of the mothers had brought a dozen slender, twisted candles in little holders of crimped tin, and while I was busy with the children, she had clipped them to the tree. She now carefully lit the candles, mindful of the paper decorations. Someone turned off the lamps, and I heard the children gasp in delight at the sight of their lovely tree. The candlelight gleamed softly on the tinfoil star and the silver ornaments, and the scent of pine drifted through the air.

Suddenly, from the back of the room, an old German grandmother began to sing "Stille Nacht." Other German voices joined in; after the first verse the words changed to "Silent Night," and everyone was singing. There were more than a few misty eyes as candles were extinguished and lamps lit.

No sooner was the room bright once again than there came a tremendous knocking at the door, and to the accompaniment of jingling sleigh bells, Santa appeared. The fact that his beard strangely resembled cotton batting and that he wore a horsehide coat instead of a red suit didn't prevent him from receiving instant recognition. He distributed the gifts the children had placed under the tree (it was simply amazing what ten cents could buy!) and presented every youngster, babies and all, with a large brown paper bag filled with a bewildering variety of candy and nuts. He also handed out my boxes of Crackerjack. Then, with much "ho, ho, ho-ing," and with more jingling of bells, he was off again, to the great relief of a few little ones.

There were cookies and popcorn balls for everyone, and the school board president passed around a box of huge, red apples. "We had enough money in our fund for these," he whispered to me.

To my embarrassed surprise, I found that Santa had left me a stack of packages — something from each family in school. The children clamored for me to open them, and proudly watched as I exclaimed over the handkerchiefs, home-made pot holders, and bottle of perfume. Never since have I received gifts offered from more generous hearts.

No one was in a hurry to leave, but at last mothers began to round up overshoes and mittens, and fathers went out to bring up the teams.

"I'm really glad we had a program," said the father who had suggested cancelling it, as he wished me a merry Christmas.

That Christmas program marked a turning point of a sort, for the weather moderated after the first of the year, and people's spirits lifted as the days warmed. Spring did not seem so far off now, and the unquenchable optimism of the farmer reasserted itself.

The schoolhouse is gone now, and so are many of the people who joined in "Silent Night" on that cold December evening. Yet each year when I hang the little silver ornaments on my tree I see once again that candle-lit room and hear the sound of singing.

Frances Wold: "The Silver Ornaments." Reprinted with permission from *Prairie Scrapbook*. Frances Wold, 1980.

The Finest Gifts

Susan Hauser

It is twenty-five below this morning. The fire in my office stove whistles earnestly and the smoke from the downstairs fire lifts from the chimney and then swirls back down around my second-story windows as though it did not quite want to go away. The dogs bark every time a house board cracks that has been bent just as far as it is willing to go and I too sit up a little, check the fires, and make sure that we are after all secure inside this tentative wooden shell.

Cold is the touchstone for true solitude, though I cannot imagine it without its twin, the blistering white snow. Today we have both, plus the pleasure of bright sun and the absence of wind, that only wants to alter things.

Yes, on a frozen day like this when even the shadows do not breathe it is easy to think that we have for a moment caught hold of time and made it stand still.

This is the perfect day, I decide, to decorate the Christmas tree. Christmas, for all its rich warmth, has a kinship to the harshest of cold: it also manages to freeze time. I pull the boxes from the shelf by the stairs, blow off the dust, and begin to unwrap the years themselves.

Each ornament has a story. As I untangle the strings and hooks I name off the people, and the places. Susan and David got this in Mexico. Aaron and Andrew made these when we lived in Bowling Green. And I made these when I was fifteen. Memory, as impossible to hold onto as smoke, becomes real in these objects. I like the feel of them in my hands, and I like the way they move on the tree, turning a little in a bit of draft when someone comes in or goes out, and doing a glad dance if someone rubs almost intentionally against the tree, the way a cat walks close by a person, but seems to not really mean to touch.

In the bottom of the ornament box I come to one of my favorite treasures: a children's book of Christmas carols. It was given to the five of us by a grandmother I do not remember and I probably would not remember the book if I had not carried it inadvertently to this place. It is illustrated with soft angel-bestrewn watercolors. There are scribbles on the inside covers, and on the back cover in bold crayon a warning: "Watch out...it might be in your bed."

Obviously it is a book that got around the house. That is why the binding is loose and the pages are frayed. But what I like best about it now is that the arrangement of the carols is so easy that even I can play them correctly on the piano. A single note for the right hand, no more than two at a time for the left. The melody emerges from behind the wooden scroll on the music ledge with the simplicity of a child's voice.

I stop decorating the tree and sit down at the piano and sing out loud, wrapping myself in the comfort of familiar words. Once again vague memory is given substance. I remember the year my mother asked my uncle to sing for her. He was too shy...embarrassed, even. But later, while she stood at the sink looking out at tree shadows stretched out long across the lake as though the sun in being so low on the horizon was pulling them beyond their means, he went down the bedroom hallway and into the bathroom and shut the door and began to sing.

"0 Holy Night," my mother's favorite. At first only a few of us heard him, but as he gathered strength from his own voice, the words overcame the natural barriers of the walls and penetrated even the farthest rooms of the house and we fell silent and were warmed and made to shiver at the same time.

I realize that my hands have stopped moving on the keys, and that I feel both warm and a little cold. I turn back to the tree. Christmas is more than a week away, but I have already opened the finest gifts.

Susan Hauser: "The Finest Gifts." Reprinted with permission from *Anna's House*, 1990. © Susan Hauser 1988.

Of Christmas Memories
and Fragrant Trees

Jack Zaleski

Artificial Christmas trees were hot items in the mid-1950s. It also was the era of plastic chairs, blond woodwork, and pink-and-grey deSotos. Tacky was the fashion. Artificial trees fit the time well. Remember?

My dad bought a fake tree. It was white, not green. There was something about a white tree that made a statement: *We* have an artificial tree. Aren't *we* the modern ones!

The white tree was part of Christmas in my parents' house for many years when I was a kid. Every year it would come out of the box, be adorned with blue ornaments and blue lights and blue tinsel. The original blue-light special.

The stiff, synthetic branches yellowed with time, and then one Christmas the fake tree was junked. My dad and I picked out a real one at a lot near the newspaper where he worked. "Trees from the Maine wood," the sign boasted. A real tree — all lush green and woodsy fragrant. It was sticky with sap and the needles stuck in our hands as we tied it into the trunk of our '53 Plymouth. I could tell my dad was having a good time.

The tree was a little crooked and lacked a branch or two on one side, but once decorated with bubble lights, shiny garland and shimmering tinsel, it was beautiful. My sister and I would sit for hours watching it sparkle in the darkened living room. When we came home from school in the afternoons the aroma of the tree would greet us as we opened the door. We knew it was Christmas. It was our job to mix sugar and water and pour it into the tree stand to keep the tree fresh. I still do that.

As I have for all the years I've lived in North Dakota, I bought a real tree this season — at one of the sales lots in Fargo-Moorhead. But there's something different about Christmas tree sales this year. A trend that started a few years ago seems to be gaining steam, and I'm not sure if it's a good thing.

I'm talking about the tendency toward homogenized trees. The promotions shout about "perfect pines," "spectacular spruces" and "fabulous firs." It's as if they're all striving for the "perfection" of artificial trees.

I stumbled around in the mud and snow in my quest for a tree, and noticed their most outstanding characteristic was manicured sameness. Designer trees. Yuck. Perfectly shaped. No bare spots, no broken branches, no crooked trunks.

At one sales place the trees had been sprayed with green stuff and they smelled like a chemical dump, not a pine forest. It should not be necessary to spray green trees green. (Yeah, I know. It's some sort of sealant to keep the tree from drying out. I still don't like it.)

I eventually found a six-foot tree — a bit bent and sporting a bare spot on one side — and took it home. When I sawed the end of the trunk off to fit it into the tree stand, I could smell the pine sap.

It's standing in the living room now, waiting to be decorated, maybe today. It draws the kids to the room. They've examined the tree from top to bottom: It's new and exciting every year.

"It's a little crooked," my son says. "Uh huh," I say, "it is." So we fiddle with the base to make it stand straight.

How's that? I ask.

"Good," he declares, feeling proud of his engineering skills.

Soon he and his sister will sit in awe as the bubble lights and shimmering tinsel throw Christmas color into the room. My sister and I felt the same way long ago. "Doesn't it smell nice," my little girl says.

Sure does. And it takes me back to that year my dad and I brought home our first real holiday tree. Every kid should have a Christmas memory like that. Mine will.

Jack Zaleski: "Of Christmas Memories and Fragrant Trees."
From *The Forum of Fargo-Moorhead*, Dec. 24, 1988.

Echoes of a Christmas

Donna M. Bosman

It's that time again...a time for steamy hot chocolate, home-made vegetable soup, and holiday preparations. It's the end of November and outside our Wisconsin home the trees glisten with the same frost that makes patterns on our windows.

Quite different from the California winters of my childhood where I always prayed for snow, if only on Christmas Eve. It never happened there, but here I can count on it.

Inside we are oblivious to the cold, as my grandsons, nine-year-old Tracy and five-year-old Todd, sip fragrant hot chocolate between turns at Chinese Checkers. I always enjoy the way the house seems to come alive with their presence. Just as it had when their mother, Jeri, was growing up.

Now Jeri is out doing some early Christmas shopping. An ideal time to put up our Christmas tree!

"Grandma, can we help please...," pleads Tracy, when I tell him of my plans. "Yeah, can we, Grandma?" Todd chimes in. "Sure" I say. "It sounds like fun."

From our walk-in attic I bring down the snow-flocked artificial tree that has been so much a part of our Christmas for twelve years. The old tree probably isn't as regal as one we might have cut down, but it enables us to put a tree up shortly before my husband, Harvey's, birthday on December 1. Then we leave it up until New Year's Day.

After struggling down the stairs with the unassembled tree in its clumsy, half-torn box, I succeed in sliding it into the living room. The boys trail behind, lured by the promise of a premature peek at Christmas-to-come.

But the children tire of hoisting the stiff, prickly branches from the box. They resume their Chinese checker game.

While I trim the tree the boys alternate squeals of delight with small quarrels as they pursue their game at the dining room table.

What seems like hours later I finish my task. "There...the tree is trimmed and ready for another year," I say to the boys as I plug in the lights. After the initial "oooo's" and "aaah's" the children's attention shifts back to their fun, and I settle down into my living room chair to survey the tree and the many decorations — survivors of Christmases long past.

My thoughts drift back to another time ... another tree ... Christmas Eve, 1945, in Torrance, California. I was nine years old and Mother and Dad and I lived in a small rented trailer home.

I was hanging fragile glass balls on the sparse little tree that the tree-lot salesman had given Dad for just hauling it away, "because," he'd said, "we probably wouldn't sell it anyway, it's such a scrawny little thing."

Times were hard for many families, ours being no exception. We couldn't *buy* a tall, stately tree, but at least we *had* a tree.

Hurriedly I put the last touches on the tree so I could finish picking up around the house before Dad brought Mother home from the bus station.

Two weeks earlier Mother had flown to a hospital in snow-laden North Dakota where my Grandma lay following a heart attack. Time was a luxury Mother could not afford.

Dad bought her a one-way plane ticket so she could fly to Fargo, but her return would have to be by bus.

The plane fare took most of our money and even our food supply was kind of small. Fortunately, Mother had made one of her army-sized batches of thick vegetable soup just the day before she was called to leave so unexpectedly.

Eventually it became catsup soup as we added water and catsup to the dwindling supply each night, but at least we weren't going hungry!

It was difficult to think of Christmas with Grandma so sick and Mother so far from home, but Dad said we should plan for the holidays because Mother would want us to. So after school I'd pick up around the trailer and then concentrate on ideas for Christmas.

Because Dad was a salesman of advertising specialties he had all kinds of neat samples. Coin purses shaped like pinwheels that opened at the squeeze of your hand. Rainbonnets that snapped together into a thin plastic ribbon to tuck neatly into your pocket or purse. Small hand mirrors, sewing kits, and Eversharp pencils with advertising on them.

Dad let me choose a few gifts from the assortment for Mother, and asked me what I'd like for myself. For my *special* gift to Mother I embroidered flowers on one of my dad's large hankies. It wasn't small and dainty, but I knew she'd like it anyway.

Dad and I wrote IOUs that promised running errands, doing dishes and other little jobs we could think of.

When we were ready, we wrapped all our offerings in cartoon sections of newspapers Mother had stored away, and we laid them neatly beneath the branches of the tree.

Then Dad left to go to the bus station to meet Mother and bring her home.

"That tree salesman would sure be surprised if he could see this 'scrawny old tree' now," I said to myself, wondering why Mother and Dad were taking so long.

Suddenly there was a thump on the side of the trailer! There they were — arms filled with what I would later discover were boxes of home-made cookies, fudge and fruitcakes made by Mother's sister from North Dakota.

I flung open the door; packages spilled down unnoticed as we hugged each other. "Merry Christmas, honey," whispered Mother. Her tear-filled eyes conveyed the tenderness we all felt at that moment.

Oh, everything was just perfect. The tree stood regally on the little end table displaying its bounteous ornaments and little heart gifts. Mother was home, Grandma was mending, and best of all, we had each other. There could be no greater gift than that.

"Grandma, why are you so sad?" asks Tracy, jolting me back to the present.

"Oh, honey, I'm not sad," I whisper as a tear slides down my cheek. "I was just thinking of a Christmas I had when I was your age. I'm happy," I say as I give both boys a hug. "And do you know why?" They shake their heads. "This will be my best Christmas ever," I smile.

("Well," I think silently, "almost....")

Donna M. Bosman is a freelance writer in Baldwin, Wisconsin.

Keeping
Christ
in
Christmas

God Is A Giver

Rev. James Bjorge

In the beginning when God created all things, He seemed to pause occasionally after sequences of creation and stand off and look it all over and then say, "That is good." Yes, it certainly was. But then God gave it to man. That was and is His nature...to give. "For God so loved the world that He gave...His only begotten Son...." (John 3:16). And Paul says, "Thanks be to God for His inexpressible gift" (II Corinthians 9:15).

God is the giver of gifts. Any person who has gotten to know God is very aware of this truth. We could even go so far as to say that God is more eager to give than we are to receive.

If it is God's nature to give and if we were created in His image...then we are going to be more God-like, fulfilled and satisfied if we, too, become givers. As Paul urges the people to help one another he says, "Remembering the words of the Lord Jesus, how He said, 'It is more blessed to give than to receive'" (Acts 20:35).

At Christmas our thoughts turn toward loved ones and there is a profusion of gifts. And everyone seems to be extra merry and happy during these festive days. Could it have anything to do with the fact that a bit of that image of God comes to life and that is very becoming to us? God gave at Christmas the greatest gift, His Son. Wise men brought their gifts from afar. And so it has gone down through the centuries with love finding expression through the means of gift-giving.

Gifts are great and giving is good. But like with most other things one can distort the whole business. Gifts can be adulterated by using them to accomplish our own purposes. They are no longer an end of love but a means for manipulation. Let's categorize them under three headings: display, didactic and dominate. When gifts are thus used they are disqualified from being genuine.

Jesus had harsh words for the Pharisees who were dedicated in giving gifts at the temple and throwing alms to the poor. It bugged Jesus because they were doing it for display. They wanted to be seen by their peers and wanted to be praised for their generosity. We still get caught in this trap of giving for show. Sometimes a man might buy his wife a corsage as they are going out for the evening, but he would not think of buying a big bouquet for the dining room table. Why? Well, everyone will see the corsage and will think what a fine, considerate husband he is.

Secondly, gifts may take on the didactic role. That is, they are used to teach a lesson or to give instruction. Perhaps a wife wants her husband to be more spiritual. She reads or hears about a book which strikes a clear note on Christian growth and commitment. She buys it, wraps it up, puts it under the Christmas tree as a present to her husband. A gift like that has the odor of foul play for the gift is being used only as an instructive tool to make the husband what she wants him to be. It violates the nature of a gift. Her motives are fine but her means are devious.

Thirdly, we give gifts to dominate. It happens not only in politics where large donations are made in order to get a piece of the elected politician and thus reap future benefits from his reign in office, but also in the daily round of gift-giving. Occasionally we bribe a child with the "dangling of the carrot" before his nose if he will practice his piano lesson or get a good grade in Latin. Now I am not saying that this kind of motivation is all bad. Not at all. But we had better not call it gift-giving. For if the child then does well, he has earned whatever we bribed him with; thus it is no longer a gift. We also succumb to the desire for power which manifests itself in giving expensive gifts so the recipient feels indebted to the giver. We know that he who pays the piper calls the tune.

So as we look at our history of gift-giving we shall probably all admit that often we have used gifts selfishly. There have been strings attached to the gift and not only on the package. But during the Christmas season I think gifts have a better chance of just being true gifts to those near and dear to us with a holy kind of carelessness; we do not give according to the merits and worthiness of our families, nor do we receive according to our just desserts. Does any parent, at Christmas shopping time, meticulously calculate the relative merits of his children and accordingly estimate how much money should be spent on each gift, following some mathematical scale of disobedience and obedience? And husbands and wives do not count up the smiles and scowls of each other and then purchase a gift that reflects the mate's merits. Instead we get caught up in the power of a great emotion, love. And love has got to express itself or it dies.

A great example of spontaneous gift-giving happened in the life of our Lord when a woman anointed him with a box of precious perfume. Some of those standing by thought it was a waste, for this expensive stuff should have been sold and the proceeds given to the poor. They said in effect, "Go easy on that perfume, sister; it costs money." But the woman forgot herself in this moment of ecstatic love and Jesus was moved. He said, "Wherever the gospel is preached in the whole world what she has done will be told in memory of her." What the woman gave was a real gift. It contained a portion of herself as she forgot herself in this glorious moment of giving.

At this sacred spot in the year called Christmas let us once again look at God's long walk down the staircase of heaven with a Baby in His arms. He came to give us redemption and life. He gives us everything that we don't deserve. He does it purely out of fatherly love with no strings attached. He wants to woo us but not manipulate us. So Christmas becomes more than Tiny Tim or a toy in a stocking, or the tinkle of bells, or steaming plum pudding. It is something about the universe. The greatest gift of all was wrapped up in a man: Emmanuel — God with us.

"For by the grace you have been saved through faith; and this is not your own doing, it is the GIFT of God — not works, lest any man should boast" (Ephesians 2:8-9). Let us accept the gift that God wants to give and do it graciously. Then the fire of love begins to burn and you feel warm all over. It is the greatest experience anyone can have. When it happens ... it transforms everything.

The book, *The Meaning of Gifts* by Dr. Paul Tournier, contains this declaration: "The great gift, the unique and living one, is not a thing but a person, It is Jesus Christ himself ... should then the little gifts of our daily existence lose their importance in the face of such a great and unique gift?" The answer comes forth with an emphatic...NO! For God's great gift can be reflected in our small gifts on earth when we give them with love...and no strings attached.

Have joy with gifts! God would have it no other way.

> How silently, how silently,
> The wondrous gift is given!
> So God imparts to human hearts
> The blessings of His heaven.

Rev. James Bjorge: "God Is a Giver." From *Howard Binford's Guide*, December 1985.

A Most Meaningful Christmas

Dee Hylden-Gronhovd

Shortly before Christmas was a poor time to be out of the mood for the Christmas spirit. Christmas is about thankfulness, about a special birthday, about wonderful things ... but I was simply missing out on the meaning just then.

I sat down to catch my breath and was suddenly back on my feet to answer the doorbell. "It's only the paper boy," I muttered as I sauntered off to get some change for the bill. Suddenly it occurred to me: He wasn't "only"; he was someone special just like everyone else.

"Maybe a nice hairdo might perk me up a bit," I thought next, testing my next approach to a good attitude. It wasn't so much the hairdo as the interesting story I read at the beauty shop that made such an impression on me that I determined to try a similar approach to making Christmas special. The article told about a family who really had a wonderful Christmas spirit. Every Christmas, the man of the house went out around the city streets to find someone who was lonely and had no place to go for the holidays. After blessing people's hearts all those years, there came a time when sadness dimmed their good intentions. The person whom they fed, clothed and even found a bed for, had been so sickly, he died during the night. The experience was so traumatic, they determined to give up the idea of helping someone each Christmas.

The more I thought about how I wished they would continue the idea of helping the poor, the more I realized that they weren't the only ones who could help the needy.

After our family discussed plans to put an ad in the paper for a free meal at Christmas to someone in need, I told the Writers Club about the idea and they agreed they would furnish cookies if we had too many people to handle. We also had the option of disconnecting the phone if things really got too overwhelming. With that in mind, we took up the challenge.

We finally got a call from a man in a run-down old hotel. He had been stranded there. He told the story of how his wife had been such a drinker, he had decided to get separated and told her he would earn money to bring his son here. Just as he had saved up enough money to call for him, he got pneumonia and used up his money on bills. Since he needed temporary help until he was strong enough to work, he decided to answer the ad to what he thought was a community service program that furnished food baskets. When he heard we were a private family he wasn't too anxious to accept. I wept when no one wanted our offer of help.

One of our sons said he would go and meet the fellow to convince him we were just trying to help. We brought him a new tie for Christmas and then he was more than willing to try this adventure. I shall never forget the scene at the old hotel — many old fellows just sitting there staring off into space on Christmas Day. What should we do?

My son and I went home to see if it would be all right with the rest of the family to bring the whole group to share our big turkey dinner. They knew it meant much to us and reluctantly agreed. We wouldn't have to eat leftovers for a week and eight people might get to enjoy Christmas a bit more. It was a great Christmas for all of us.

We had also invited some friends to help us entertain our strange guests. Christmas Day took on a special glow! I wouldn't have cared if all the strangers had lice. It was well worth the risk to see the look of delight on their faces when they all sat down to dinner.

What a blessing! All our other friends, great as they were, couldn't have begun to do as much for our happiness that Christmas morning.

Our family had a great time finding some warm clothing to give them. The visitors were a delight.

One fellow, almost ninety years of age, could still joke. He had a homemade hearing aid composed of approximately two feet of clear plastic hose with a funnel on the end. He claimed it worked better than those you buy. My response, "that's just great," reverberated through his listening contraption. The jolly old fellow stated that it was the first time in thirty years he'd been invited to dinner and claimed, "I think I'll return to my wife if home cooking is like this." I wasn't sure that should be the reason to have a wife, but we enjoyed seeing him happy. His frequent expression was, "This is great!"

Another highlight of that adventurous day was when one of the men, who seemed to have chosen a wrong way to drown his troubles by a few drinks before he came, decided he would like to say a table prayer. It seemed more sincere than that of most folks and I'm sure it didn't go unheard.

When I realized that most anyone can get into negative situations by circumstances beyond control, it made me feel very happy to cheer up a few folks that Christmas day of long ago — that very special Christmas day.

Dee Hylden-Gronhovd is a freelance writer from Grand Forks, North Dakota.

Special Feelings of Christmas

Alexander F. Stoffel

The colors are so warm and bright that they seem to fill my person from the inside out. The beautiful greens of the long needles of the Norway pine seem a perfect complement to the golds, reds, blues, yellows, and who-can-count-how-many-other colors reflected by the decorations hanging on it. That smell I remember so well from my youngest days — the smell of good pine needles mixes with and is finally overpowered by the wonderful aroma of the roasting turkey in the oven.

My eyes turn to the mountain of brightly-decorated presents heaped under the tree until it seems that there can be no room for more, not even one. The children have been eyeing them separately and in groups all day, hardly being able to wait for the meal to be completed so that they can begin to open them and discover the wonders they have been anticipating for these past few weeks. Their excitement is infectious, and soon I am caught up in it.

Most of the family is together, and those who cannot be here have been in contact several times in recent days by phone and by mail, so it *feels* as if everyone is here even if they're not. And there were all those cards, sometimes from people we considered very good friends, sometimes those whom time and distance removed from our immediate thoughts during the rest of the year.

It has been several weeks of "Merry Christmas" and "Happy Holidays" chanted frequently almost in reflex to people we know, as well as to people we have never seen before and probably never will again. And the music, always the beautiful and well-remembered carols, surrounds us and massages us until finally we join in and we, too, soar to heights of feelings of good cheer and good will to all in the world.

There have been church Christmas programs and school Christmas programs and Christmas programs by just about every possible organization known to civilized man. We watched with baited breath for a little child to speak his/her short line in a stammering voice, starting and stopping in fits of a faulty memory, only to ultimately realize that it didn't matter because he/she was so cute struggling with pronouncing "frankincense" or some such word.

Christmas will be, for us, a worship of God and the Son He gave to the world. For a time, we will have hope for a better life for all than was experienced last year, hope for peace and good will among men, hope for the love of God to take root in hearts hitherto impregnable to the onslaught of the Holy Spirit. Truly, it is a season of joy, of hope, of life, of love, even (in spite of all the rushing about) of peace.

I go to the window and look out. It is cold out there. There isn't all that much snow this year, but there is really a bite to the wind. And suddenly the contrast of it all hits me, the cold out there and the warm in here. This, I realize, is much more the way it really is than I want to believe. Perhaps I have too eagerly shut out the memories and the faces of the others from the past Christmases. And it all comes back to me in a deluge of mental pictures from long ago.

I see the misery in the eyes of a young man standing on an ice-cold, wind-swept street corner. He is telling me of the current status of a custody battle for his children, the result of a divorce he doesn't want. A prominent member of the community passes us, and smiling warmly, says, "Merry Christmas." The young man hesitates as he pulls his thoughts together to focus on the intrusion. Automatically, he smiles and responds, as do I. "Merry Christmas," he says, and then his eyes slowly dim and he sinks back into the despair he so obviously feels inside. His shoulders are now hunched up to ward against the cold ... or maybe it isn't the cold alone.

The image in my mind turns to a woman of some sixty-plus years with whom I visited. Her eyes are stark with the pain of grief, for she lost her husband no more than four months back. For the first time in more than forty years, she will be alone at Christmas ... well, not physically alone, because she will be with children and grandchildren. They, too, had their grief, and they worked so hard to lift her up. She can't cry in their presence because it would hurt them too much and maybe even spoil their Christmas, so she doesn't. She smiles and bakes cookies even though in her heart it is a sickening sham. She cries when she talks to me, though, huge wrenching sobs boiling up out of all of the fear and anger and misery within her.

Oh, I can remember all the others.... There are so many of them, that's what overwhelms me.

There's the young woman who no longer knows who she is because her husband has found another. She has to wear her mask for the sake of the children, and she has no place and no time to work out her grief. Sometimes I can see her in a store. She is brightly smiling and greeting others at every hand. I wonder, how many know the lie of her smile?

Oh, yes, there's the middle-aged man who just lost his job because the company he worked for retooled, and now he has no skills to market. I see him in a large discount store. He is standing there with a resolute face, but I can almost hear him wondering how he is going to pay for the presents he feels obligated to buy. And he wonders what is left to his life. But there, see it? He smiles when the checkout clerk greets him with Christmas cheer. He responds in kind.

Carol (the name I made up, the person I didn't) comes to mind. She is a woman trapped by the biochemical imbalances of her body. Menopause has struck with untold viciousness, and the medical science of that day cannot as readily alleviate it as it can today. She is confused about her life and incredibly depressed. Christmas is, for her, a worse nightmare than you or I will ever experience in our sleep. She is a living, breathing scream of depressed and fearful agony, but existing in a time and place where if she does anything less than smile and offer apparently heart-felt Christmas greetings, she will be ostracized and rejected by the very people she grimly hangs on to for a smallest part of stability. Carol has a choice. She can be out and among people, masking her depression under a few layers of lies, or she can stay home away from people. If she does the latter, however, people will talk about her. So, she compromises, going out as often as she can, but hiding at home when she can't do it anymore. She truly loathes Christmas for no other reason than that she must then lie more to the world than at any other time of the year.

With the passing of the image of Carol, the flow of mental pictures stops. I feel drained. I remember that once there was a great preacher who used to stand in the pulpit silently just before beginning his sermon. He would say some words to himself (I do not know from whence they came): "Never morning wore to evening but some heart did break." So much truth. We are surrounded by broken people, and perhaps it is even true that we, who cannot see the broken people, are the most broken of all.

Well, this is a really sad and depressing view of Christmas, isn't it? I mean, that's the way the world is, isn't it? Are we supposed to let the fact that misery abounds in an imperfect world spoil our own joyous celebration? Though being ourselves more or less intact, must we drown in the pain of others?

I don't know. I wonder, this is the season we celebrate the coming of the Christ, the outpouring of God's love. He who came, what would He do? Would He demand that everyone smile so that our joy is not marred? Would He ignore misery so that bright colors, happy songs, and cheerful voices could abound? Would He permit pain to be magnified out of all understanding as the price for a superficial warm glow in the pits of our stomachs? Somehow I think not.

Maybe we need to emphasize a little less the trappings of His coming and focus a little more upon *why* He came and *what* He came to do. If He came to bring love into our lives, how can we turn our backs upon it?

Perhaps it might be possible to watch, this Christmas, with eyes that are not afraid to see pain, to hear with ears tuned for a cry for help, with arms ready to embrace not only children and loved ones,

A Merrie Prairie Christmas

but also those who need comfort. Perhaps we might close our judging minds for a moment, and not condemn a word or a feeling expressed in a way which might dampen *our* joy. Sometimes, I think, we sing so loudly because we are afraid to hear the soft agony all around us. Maybe, just maybe, we may learn not only to sing more softly, but also to see through our own smiles.

We can't solve all of the problems of people in this world. No one (other than God) can. But we can listen ... and touch ... and reach out with our hearts. We might even find that love pouring through us to others *does* heal, that it *can* bring peace, not only to them, but also to us.

Wouldn't that be wonderful? Maybe then we could understand what Christmas really is. We might understand Christmas in the context of the world instead of just our close family circles. Unbelievable! We could sing "Joy to the World," and not only really mean it, but also understand it.

And then maybe some of our Christmas joy could be a little less self-indulgent. Who knows? It might even last into the next year.

Alexander F. Stoffel: "Special Feelings of Christmas." Stoffel is a writer who lives in Fargo, North Dakota.

The UFO

Jim Baccus

"I want to make a report," the herdsman said.

He stood before the officer with his battered hat in his hand, his face pale and intent.

Ye gods, another one, the deputy thought. These hill and pasture people....

His cramped office had seen other visitors this night, until it was redolent of cattle and unwashed bodies. The deputy's own socks stank in his boots and his weapon hung heavily on his shoulders. He was hungry and tired and drawing a graveyard shift.

"You rednecks have been drinking out of the tabasco bottle again," the officer said cruelly. As always, most of the rumor-mongers, the unidentified-flying-object and bright-light sighters, didn't seem to have a full set of dishes.

"No," the herdsman said. "It came down and shone right in my face. I saw it with my own eyes. It blinded me for a minute. Then I saw it go back in the sky."

"You saw it go back in the sky. Any green men with long noses hop out? Reconnoitering, mebbe — looking over the landscape to make a landing? Planning how to drop a squadron or two and conquer the country?"

"I don't know," The herdsman said. He seemed muted and sad.

"Would you tell me," the officer said, "why anybody would want to capture this miserable country that even the gods forgot?"

"It frightened me," the visitor said. "There have been rumors..."

"Rumors, schumers," the deputy said. He found himself wondering what his wife was doing this cold night. After a pause he said: "Well, what do you want me to do?"

"I don't know," the man said again.

"Look," the deputy said. "We've had these rumors for a long time now. Nothing came of them. You saw a blinding light, then it dwindled, took off into the sky. I'll make a report."

He found the report form, not the first one he'd prepared. Tomorrow the lieutenant would frown when he saw the pile of paperwork. Reluctantly he took up a pen.

"Now. This thing that came out of the sky and blinded you. Did it say anything?"

"No. But maybe it was a warning," the herdsman said. "Maybe we are being warned about our sins."

"You hill people sure got some weird religions," the deputy said. "We'll put down you saw a blinding light that went back into the sky."

Slowly he put it down, pausing to rub his eyes. When he turned back again he saw his visitor was gone. Disgustedly he crumpled the report form, threw it on the floor, hawked and spat on it. Behind him, the door scraped.

By the gods, another visitor! But this one was no shepherd, no goatherd. They regarded each other. "Propertius, a traveler," the newcomer said at last. He accent was unfamiliar.

"Phocion. In charge of Judea Township — for tonight, anyway," the deputy said.

"Ah. This is Bethlehem. Will you point me toward the stables?"

"The stables?" the centurion repeated. Something about the man's grave manner and steady eye pulled Phocion to his feet. His sword clanked against the table.

"Ah...stables, sir. They're just on the other side of the inn. You'll find them easy. You run into them at the end of the road."

Jim Baccus: "The UFO." From *I'm Thinking It Over*, North Dakota Institute for Regional Studies, 1987.

Christmas

Fresh yet familiar,
giving more than it
takes away, too
much for one,
enough for all ....
Christmas is the always
we wish each other.

— Y. 1985

Christmas After

God bless this tree, tomorrow down,
bless those who trimmed it, too:
our little time for fantasy
and far too much to do.

Store safe these boxes, oddly-shaped,
loved ornaments and new,
and treasure quick-scrawled "fragile," "lites,"
by hands that loved us true.

In homes at peace this Christmas night,
let hearts cheered through and through
allow each moment bitter, sweet,
warm Christmas after, too.

— Y. 1986

Yvonne Hunter is a writer from Minneapolis, Minnesota.

Holiday Traditions

Der Nikolaus Is Coming!

Julie Welle Verzuh

This year would be the best. I was twelve and I could easily play the part of Christmas Past in the condensed version of Dickens' *Christmas Carol*, or Mrs. McGregor in the one-act play Miss Peters had sent for called *Cooking the Goose*, or even the Virgin Mary in the tableau. Just so Joe Klaus didn't get to play Joseph. That would spoil everything for me.

It would be just like the teacher to give him the part because he had that consistently simple look on his face that she mistook for holiness. The rest of us knew what lurked underneath that shock of red-gold hair. We were all looking forward to *der Nikolaus* and his *Knecht* arriving on the night of the school program, wondering if Joe Klaus could stand up to St. Nick.

The week after Halloween all of the parts were handed out. Joe Klaus did not get Joseph. Miss Peters did give me the part of Mrs. McGregor, but she gave the part of Mary to Christine. However, she had changed the tableau this year and written a special part for the Angel — the one that said, "Fear not..." to the shepherds. That she gave to me because she wanted me to sing the words to the tune of "Hark the Herald Angels Sing," with a few liberties taken here and there. I couldn't believe it! I didn't even know I could sing. I mean, we always sang at home, at school, and at church, and discovering the joy of music was one of the Big Discoveries of Life for me. But now I was going to be *a singer!*

The night of the performance came ever closer. Each child in the thirty-six total school population had at least two different dramatic assignments, and we respected Miss Peters for being fair. The four first graders, five second graders, and five third graders had each memorized rhymes for a letter to spell out Merry Christmas. The fourth through eighth would present group songs, choral readings, and plays. Mothers were sewing muslin sheets together for curtains which would be strung on a wire across the front of the schoolroom. Josie, who was clever at that sort of thing, had constructed a magnificent pair of wings for me. She had bent two large wire coat hangers in the shape of wings and stretched white cheesecloth over them. The tips were fashioned out of elongated cardboard cones attached with needle and thread, and covered over with the same white "mix" we used for building relief maps. With a sash that tied high around by bodice, the wings were fastened securely to by body. I tried on the entire costume including the halo upstairs in the girls' bedroom in front of the dresser mirror. When I stood on a chair I could see the full length of me, and I looked truly heavenly — even supernatural!

At seven o'clock on the evening of the twelfth of December the parents brought their children to school, sat in their desks, and waited patiently for the program to begin, passing the time between themselves in earnest conversation. Behind the curtain there was a constant hum punctuated by something dropping now and then, regular hisses of "sh-h-h," and shuffling of feet.

The lower grades were first. Each child pulled his large red construction paper letter from behind his back and held it high above, all of them together trying to make a reasonably horizontal line. At the end each ran to the parents with the gift of the letter and themselves to sit with them for the rest of the show. One of the younger children had caught a cold, and so our precocious Annie obliged by doing two letters, and that caused a titter among the audience as she first did one, then the other, holding the first with the right hand, and the second with the left.

Everything went in order without a disaster until Miss Peters attempted to attach my wings for the tableau. Of course we were crowded backstage which was a small space on either side of the "stage." She reached for the wings that were lying on top of the bookcase which was the school library. But her fingers flew too fast as she tried to set the appendages on my back. She bent one of the wings, and when she tried to bend it back, she ripped the cheesecloth. I spread my long blond hair carefully with my fingertips, and when my cue came, I stood a little sideways, trying to conceal the battered and drooping wing, but the audience noticed and could not stifle their amusement. Afterwards, I couldn't remember if I sang well or not.

But it was over. Everyone was making way for *der Nikolaus*. They had gathered us all in the front again to be properly ready for his visit. Someone thought he saw a team of horses and a sleigh pull up outside, or a flash of red go past a window, but no one dared to look — not even the eighth grade boys. They were nervously talking in loud voices to one another though, bragging about how *Nikolaus* would never make them kneel.

The suspense was broken by a loud nerve-shattering THUMP, THUMP, THUMP — the ominous sound of a long large branch that had been yanked off a tree and now was being stomped on the wooden floor of the entry. I flew to Annie's side and held her trembling hand as the door was flung open. I bent down and whispered to her, "Er tut dir nicht weh." ("He will not hurt you.") I saw Mama glance at me appreciatively. Only six days ago, on his feast day, *der Nikolaus* had left Annie (and all of us) fruits and nuts on the porch;

but we had heard some boys in the neighborhood had gotten switches in gunny sacks instead. Girls naturally behaved better than boys and *der Nikolaus* knew everything.

His *Knecht* came first — a dwarfish figure dressed all in black with a hood over his head, only the ghastly face mask showing. In his hand he carried a horse whip, and he looked like *der Teufel* (the Devil) himself. Everyone shrank back as he moved forward. *Nikolaus* was not far behind, a contrast to his servant — tall, lean, and almost entirely red, including a ruddy garish face mask. His white beard was thin and scraggly. He bore no resemblance to the kind bishop of legendary fame, or to the Santa Claus in commercial advertisements we saw in magazines, or to the Santa in Annie's coloring book. Our *Nikolaus* was a disciple of a fearsome God who punished children when they were not good, and rewarded them if they were not bad.

Nikolaus struck his tree scepter on the floor again and spoke, "Singt jetzt die Weinachtslieder." ("Now sing the Christmas songs.") With lusty voices we sang as we had been instructed: the *Tannenbaum* song, "Ihr Kinderlein Kommet," "Jingle Bells," and finally "Jolly Old St. Nicholas." When it came to the part in the song that went "down through the chimney with good St. Nick," Joe Klaus yelled out clearly, "...with a good swift kick!" *Der Knecht* pulled him by his hair from the back row and snapped his whip in the air over him.

Der Nikolaus commanded, "Kneel!"

Joe Klaus would not kneel.

Der Nikolaus struck him on the shoulder with his branch. Louder this time, he said again, "Kneel!"

Joe Klaus would not kneel.

That was enough. *Der Knecht* picked him up bodily and carried him out. Joe did not struggle. His face was white. He made no sound, but from where most of us stood we could see a dark spot on the front of his good wool pants. *Nikolaus* then pointed his stick at Frank (the Ox) Brunnen and asked him to say a "Hail Mary," which he did in a quavering voice, starting over when he stumbled.

In the end *der Nikolaus* reached in his bag and handed out small paper sacks to each child as each came forward and said, "Thank you." I went with Annie.

At home I cracked open the nuts with a hammer. My mind was turning over and over but this Saint made no sense. "Macht nichts aus," (no matter) I finally thought. Now we would wait for *das Cristkinje* to arrive on the twenty-fourth of December — the God-Child Himself who was sweet and kind and loving, and made us all feel warm inside.

Julie Welle Verzuh: "Christmas Plays." From *From the Heart of Lizzie*. North Star Press, 1983.

Anna's Christmas

Anna Guttormsen Hought with Florence Ekstrand

If there was one time of the year when we had foods that were very special, it was at Christmas time. Mother had a word for it then: *Ach mej!* It was an expression of great satisfaction. "*Ach mej!* Doesn't that cake look fine?"

Preparations for Christmas started early. We began to feel the excitement when Mother began cleaning house. Everything had to be scrubbed, including the plain wooden chairs with their many rungs. The curtains were all washed, starched, and ironed. They smelled so fresh and good! Mother thought it was important that everything smell fresh and clean.

We baked every kind of little cookies, or *småkakar — fattigmand, berliner kranser, sirupskaka* (molasses cookies). None were eaten before Christmas. We even baked little cookies for Mimi, the cat, and hung them low on the tree.

The boys went up into the woods to cut a Christmas tree for us. Sometimes, if the snow wasn't too deep, I could go along. We trimmed the tree with lots of cookies, woven paper baskets filled with candy and nuts and with our names on them, paper stars and tinsel and rope.

But the candles on the tree were not to be lighted until after our Christmas Eve supper. That evening we started with rommegrøt, a rich milk, cream and flour pudding, like a soup course. After that came pork ribs and potatoes. We always had a rice pudding with an almond hidden in it; the one who got the nut would be the next one married.

There was never much in the way of gifts and the gifts we did get were usually very practical. But the year that Oscar was five he got a toboggan. He was so excited that he sat on it all evening and no one could get him off it. I got an apron that same year and my brother John liked it so well he wore it all evening. It was at Christmas I gave my mother the *sukker og fløte* doily. And the year I was fifteen I started to make her a Hardanger-embroidered tablecloth a yard square. It was for the table in the living room, over which hung a lamp that pulled up and down, with prisms underneath. The cloth (which got finished just in time for Mother's birthday in May) was laid over a plush tablecloth with fringes, and a plant was set in the middle.

One year when I was quite small, I had seen a miniature mask made of marzipan candy in a shop window. I was fascinated by it.

How I wanted that tiny mask! It cost perhaps twenty-five cents, but I didn't have the money. So I begged Mother to give me the marzipan mask for Christmas.

"You have plenty," said Mother. But I begged (I might say "pestered") her until she gave in and gave me twenty-five cents. I ran to the store and bought the candy mask. I brought it home and it was hung on the Christmas tree, which we were not allowed to see until Christmas Eve.

Meanwhile, Mother and Father had invited guests for Christmas Eve. Down the road a way lived a woman who worked in the brewery, and more often than not sampled the wares. Father met her on the road one day and asked her if they would be having a Christmas, but she said no, that wasn't likely. It was always the custom to invite anyone in the community who might not otherwise have a festive Christmas, so Mother and Father invited the two young daughters of this woman to spend Christmas Eve with us.

We had eaten our lovely meal, we had danced around the tree, we had sung our Christmas songs. Now it was time for Father to *hoste Jule-tre*, to take the goodies off the tree and distribute them among us. One by one he gave the sweets to each of us children. At last — oh, at last! — he came to the marzipan mask! He picked it off the tree.

"Oh, it's too bad we don't have one for each of you girls," he said, turning to the two visiting girls. "Instead you will have to divide this between you."

I thought I would faint. My marzipan mask! I turned and met Mother's eyes, and while I bit my tongue and said nothing, the look said, "That was mine!"

Mother only gave me a long look. "You will have to learn to share," she said.

On Christmas Day we had another big meal at noon and then we were supposed to rest. To a child that was the worst thing that could have happened. What a waste of time! Sometimes we would be allowed to use our skis a little. But Mother was intent on getting us to rest. She probably thought all the excitement of Christmas was too much for us!

Anna Guttormsen Hought with Florence Ekstrand: "Anna's Christmas." From *Anna: Norse Roots in Homestead Soil.* Welcome Press, 1986.

Mommy's Christmas Roses

Merry Ann Reitmeier-Grove

When my fourth son Tyler was three years old, he was painfully shy. We gently called him "Shy Ty." He rarely caused a stir, and I do not recall ever having to spank him. So you can imagine our shock when we found him standing by the Christmas tree with tears in his big brown eyes, looking absolutely miserable. I kneeled and softly asked, "Sweetheart, what's the matter?"

Tears sliding down his cheeks, he sobbed, "Where is you Cissmus woses?"

I was quite sure he did not know what Christmas roses were. I asked, "Tyler, what do Christmas roses look like?" He replied adamantly, "Oh, you know!"

He was sobbing out loud now, so the rest of the family came into the living room. One of his brothers got the Christmas catalog and stared pointing out objects. "Tyler, is this Mommy's Christmas roses?" he would ask. Tyler let us know all the things that they were not. He didn't eat supper that night, and was despondent. At bedtime,as he was drifting off to sleep I heard him softly sigh, "Fin' Mommy's Cissmus woses."

We thought he would forget overnight. Not so. At breakfast he said, "C'mon, Papa, go chopping." As we'd exhausted every possible idea to find out what his little mind thought was a Christmas rose, we decided to humor him. After going through several stores, and after the poor little guy was asked a hundred times if *this*, at last, was Mommy's Christmas roses, Tyler found them. His father said he pointed to them and shouted, "Dare dey are!"

The clerk took them down and handed them to Tyler. He paid for them himself and put them in the sack. He hugged the sack all the way home.

When he came into the kitchen he simply said, "I foun' 'em." Without removing his "Minnesota winter warmth," he marched into the living room, plunked down under the tree, opened his sack, and very tenderly placed his treasure beneath the tree. The lights sparkled in his smiling brown eyes as he declared, "Mommy's Cissmus woses!" His brothers, his father and I all agreed that Tyler's green plastic ring of holly with red berries was the most beautiful Christmas roses we'd ever seen. It was Christmas Eve.

The $1.29 ring is gone, and the incident was more or less forgotten until Tyler's seventeenth Christmas. By then he'd grown into the type of young man who makes you wish you had ten more just like him.

Last year, with only his brother Kym and me at home, Tyler hugged me from behind as I played Christmas music on the organ. Clutched in his man-sized hand was a perfect long-stemmed red rose.

The tears welled up in my eyes as I whispered to no one, "Mommy's Cissmus woses." I could barely talk as I told them the story they did not recall having ever heard before. When I finished, we all had "happy drops" in our eyes.

Merry Ann Reitmeier-Grove lives in Crookston, Minnesota.

Julebuk

Erling Nicolai Rolfsrud

With the onset of frigid weather, Sara's father decided to trap and hunt as his brother had done. He set traps for muskrats and mink, and whenever he went out to check his traps, he carried Will's rifle for a chance shot at a skulking coyote. Nearly every time he returned from his traps, he brought several muskrats, and now and then a mink. Sara learned to help with the distasteful chore of skinning. She held the leg or tail, while her father deftly stripped the pelt off. One day he came home with a coyote slung over his shoulder, and again Sara helped him with the skinning. Since Papa had no son to help him, she worked with him as much as she disliked the job. "In winter," Mr. Miller told her, "the fur is in prime condition, and we get the best market price."

Winter days followed a routine — barn chores in the morning and evening, hunting and trapping for Mr. Miller during the day, studies and organ lessons for Sara, housekeeping, cooking and teaching for Mrs. Miller. Once a week Margit came on her home-made skis and learned more English.

After the electric lights of their home in Alexandria, the Millers found their kerosene lamps shed such dim light they retired early in the evening. "Best to get up with the chickens and go to bed with the chickens," Mr. Miller decided.

During very cold weather, Sara often awakened to hear her father putting more coal in both stoves. Snuggled under several quilts, she felt comfortable. But the loft window nearby thickened with heavy frost.

One evening after Christmas, the Miller family heard the jangling of harness tug links, hoof beats muffled in the snow, and the swooshing of sled runners. Soon there came a rapping at the door, and when Mr. Miller opened it, the three Millers stared dumb-founded as little and big persons trooped inside, each wearing paper sacks over their heads. They stood in silence, answering nothing to Mr. Miller's "Well, hello. What is this? Who are you?"

Minutes passed. No one stirred. Dressed in old and ill-fitting garments, the visitors stood like ridiculous statues. Then one in man's clothing stepped out before the rest and danced a jig. When he stopped, Sara heard a familiar titter.

"Margit!" she exclaimed.

Off came the paper mask to reveal a grinning Margit. Mr. Miller turned to her and asked, "Margit, what is this?"

"Yulebuk," Margit answered.

"Well, what is *Yulebuk*?"

"Oh, it is fun ve have at Yule time. Ve dress funny. You are supposed to guess the name of each vun. Vhen you guess right, he take off his mask."

Sara spotted a tuft of red hair sticking through a torn paper sack. The boy who wore it fit the size of Gunnar Hagen.

"Gunnar!" she called, coming toward him and pointing at him. Then in succession, judging by their heights, she identified Gunnar's brother Magnus, then Olaf and Nils Lund. "Where is Mikkel?" she asked Nils.

"He stay home with Mama and Baby. But Papa he come." By this time Mrs.

Miller had identified Elsa and Mrs. Anderson, but two men and one woman remained a puzzle. Again, the same man stepped out and jigged.

Sara recalled that once during recess, Magnus had tried to dance a jig with Elsa. His father must have taught him. So now Sara pointed to the jigging man and said, "Mr. Hagen," and twirling around to the masked woman, she said, "And you must be Mrs. Hagen."

Glad to get out of her warm mask, Mrs. Hagen reached a hand to Mrs. Miller. "Nice to meet you."

The remaining masked man stood by the door which now opened to admit another man with paper sack over his head. Olaf spoke to Mr. Miller. "He un-hitch horses. Now you guess who he is. You know him good."

Mr. Miller looked carefully at the slightly stooped man. Sara stared, not daring to believe that the man wearing the paper mask could be Simon Larson, yet he had the same halting walk, the same size.

She touched her father's arm. "That looks like it could be Mr. Larson," she whispered.

For answer her father chuckled and called out, "Simon, you can quit hiding under that paper sack!"

And the paper sack came off to reveal Simon Larson, grinning rather bashfully.

Olaf called to the man standing at the door. "Papa he the last vun nobody guess." And he motioned to his father to remove the paper bag.

As each person had been identified, the warm clothes were shed. Now Mrs. Anderson held out a book to Mrs. Miller. "You play organ. Ve sing! Ve sing!"

Mrs. Miller accepted the book and saw that it was a Norwegian song book. Mrs. Anderson kept nodding her head, her eyes shining. "You play music. Ve sing." She turned the page to a familiar Christmas carol.

Mrs. Miller played the first bars and Sara immediately recognized the well known "Silent Night, Holy Night." And now all their Norwegian neighbors joined in singing:

> Glade jul, hellige jul.
> Engle daler ned i skjul.
> Hid de flyver med paradis-gront.
> Hvor de ser, hvad for Gud er skjont.
> Lonlig iblandt os de gaar,
> Lonlig iblandt os de gaar.

Erling Nicolai Rolfsrud: "Julebuk." Reprinted with permission of the author from *Cutbank Girl*. © Erling Nicolai Rolfsrud 1985.

A Merrie Prairie Christmas

St. Lucia Day and Beyond

Florence Ekstrand

When the harvest was at last finished, when the flax was in the drying shed, when the last threshing floor had been swept and the grain was ready for the mill, darkness and cold were already setting in. On St. Simon's Day, October 28 according to the calendar stick, the cattle were to be moved indoors for the winter. On St. Martin's Day, November 11, any farm animals that were not to be kept through the winter should be slaughtered — all, that is, except the Christmas pig. On St. Catherine's Day, November 25, women of the house should begin their spinning for the winter. On St. Thomas' Day, December 21, the Christmas ale should be brewed.

But eight days before that, on December 13, came the day that marked the start of the Christmas preparations — St. Lucia's Day.

So familiar is the Lucia Day festivity in this country that we forget the festival as we know it is of fairly recent origin.

But like many other festivals its roots are in ancient times. Under the old calendar, the night of December 13 was considered the longest night of the year. Horrible beings from the bowels of the earth were believed to be afoot that night and the early Norsemen feasted and drank in their effort to call forth the sun god again. Soon they themselves began to dress in grotesque masks and strange clothes and went about frightening as many poor souls as they could. Their refreshments at the homes where they called were not coffee and Lucia buns, but *brannvin* (brandy) — *lussesup* (literally "cup of light"). Over the years it became the custom to serve this "cup of light" to the butcher, for this was the day on which he came to stick the Christmas pig.

How this old celebration of light merged with the legend of St. Lucia of Sicily is hard to say. Lucia, a beautiful young woman of Syracuse, was born in 283 and was converted to Christianity. When her mother fell ill, it is told, Lucia made a vow that if God would spare her mother's life she would forego marriage and remain a virgin. When her mother recovered, Lucia persuaded her to divide among the poor all the wealth and possessions that would have been Lucia's dowry.

Furious, the man to whom she was engaged reported her to the authorities. Since she was without dowry, they sought to force her into prostitution. Remarkable, she remained a virgin and even survived burning at the stake. But in the year 303 she died by the executioner's sword.

Did the Vikings bring back the tales of Lucia? Did the early missionaries tell her story? Was it the similarity between her name and the word for light (*ljus*) that drew the Scandinavians, especially the Swedes, so deeply to her legend? One of the tales most often told is that during a famine in Varmland a brightly lighted ship came sailing in on Lake Venern. It was Lucia, bringing vast gifts of good. Was it the memory of the pagan goddess Freya, who was said to bring mead in a golden horn as harbinger of a good year to come?

Although there are records of earlier observances, the custom of the eldest daughter of the house serving coffee and saffron buns on the morning of December 13 seems to have started around 1700 among rich farmers and estate owners in west Sweden. At first Lucia was depicted as an angel with wings, but in time she was simply the eldest daughter in a white gown with a crown of blazing candles on her head. From there the custom spread. Today many churches and lodges in United States and Canada hold Lucia fests.

Whatever the origins, in its present form it is a charming family observance. It is a time to pause in what has become a hectic race before Christmas. It is a glance back at a simpler time, a sharing, an expression of love and a harbinger of the real Festival of Light.

By St. Lucia's Day, any farm work to be done before Christmas was to be completed. Now the preparations began inside the house.

Writing for a Stockholm newspaper, *Dagens Nyheter*, Lars-Ingmar Karlsson recently interviewed two elderly sisters who grew up many years ago on a large farm in Halland in southern Sweden. Their account of getting ready for Christmas is probably much like that your grandmother would have told you.

Since they had help both in the house and with the cattle, Astrid and Nanny explained, the people of the household usually handled all the work alone. But early in December it was time to do one of the biggest clothes washings of the year and so the "washer-women" came. Each of these two women lived alone in a small *stuga* in the neighborhood and made the rounds of the farms, "helping out."

The washing took two full days. On the first day they scrubbed the clothes, standing at a large tub filled with steaming hot water. By evening they moved the clothes into a huge round tub, big as a dining table, and there they soaked overnight. In the morning the water was poured out and the tub loaded on a wagon and hauled to a nearby spring where the water ran even through the snow. Here the clothes were rinsed, then brought home to hang on lines and fences to freeze dry.

Next came the butchering. Always before Christmas a pig must be butchered and often a calf as well.

"Part of the meat went into sausage," Astrid recalled. "There was meat sausage and blood sausage and a few other kinds of sausage.

The meat *korv* was salted down and later hung on long poles either in the pantry or the kitchen."

"The blood sausage was especially good," Nanny put in, "and we ate that up in a hurry!"

The old saying about using every bit of the pig but the squeal was certainly true. "We made *sylta* of the cooked head. The liver was either cooked or made into liver sausage or paté. But one part of the pig that was never eaten at Christmas was the ham. It was salted down along with much of the meat in a huge barrel. Some of the salted meat might be brought out at Christmas, but the rest was always saved until spring, even into the summer."

After the butchering came the baking. "Mama would say, 'Now it's time to go get flour,'" Nanny remembered, "and off we went to the mill to get our grain ground. We baked *matbrod* (the regular dark mealtime bread), *smakakor* (little cookies) and *pepparkakor* (ginger cookies)."

It was almost Christmas now, and time to scrub the whole house from top to bottom. When it was shining clean and smelling of strong homemade soap, the new rag rugs were laid down, the ones their mother had been weaving all fall and winter on her noisy loom. (In earlier times small, snipped cedar twigs were strewn over the floor.)

But there was one chore left.

"The day before Christmas Eve," smiled Astrid, "a big tub was set out near the stove and filled with water. One after another, each in our turn, we children hopped into the tub and got a good scrubbing."

"And when we woke up on Christmas Eve," continued Nanny, "we saw the beautiful new curtains that had been hung up during the night."

Both agreed that gifts were never important.

"It wasn't always that we were given gifts," Astrid recalled. "But if we were it was something practical, like mittens and stockings. Sometimes we wished that once we should get something that wasn't so useful."

"But," added Nanny, "the best part about Christmas was, after all, the good food."

An elderly Norwegian friend agreed that gifts were never an important part of Christmas.

"The special thing," she remembered, "was that we were all at home together. While my mother cooked rice pudding for Christmas Eve, my father read stories to us children. This is the thing I remember most."

By the Julian calendar, Christmas fell on January 6, thirteen days later than our present Christmas. In times past — and to a certain extent today — the celebrating of Christmas went on through that whole time. The Church may, in fact, have had to take a hand in bringing the feasting and drinking to an end.

For the folklore and church lore accompanying the Norwegian calendar stick gives January 6 as the day on which ends the Christmas celebration proper. On St. Brictiva's Day, January 11, all the leftovers from the Christmas feasting were to be mixed together and eaten up, and all the Christmas ale was to be drunk up. Neighbors went from place to place helping with the clean-up.

Finally, on January 13, the Twentieth Day of Christmas, the church bells pealed out a warning that the celebrating was over and it was time to get back to work.

This was the day the farmers and their hired hands were to begin chopping timber to add to the dwindling woodpile. The year had come full circle.

Florence Ekstrand: "St. Lucia Day and Beyond." From *Notes From a Scandinavian Parlor*. Welcome Press: 1984.

Lucia Buns

Heat 2 1/2 cups milk to lukewarm. Dissolve in it 3 envelopes dry yeast, 1/2 cup butter, 1/2 teaspoon saffron, 1 1/2 teaspoon salt, 1 1/2 cups sugar. Add about 4 cups flour, 1 egg, beaten; 1 cup raisins, 1/2 cup blanched and chopped almonds. Beat this thoroughly into a light dough, then add gradually another 4 cups of flour, just enough to make a dough that handles well. Knead it until smooth. Let rise double. Now work in another half cup of soft butter until thoroughly blended. Put dough on floured board, let rest 10 minutes, then shape into buns. Let rise on buttered cookie tin until light and almost double in size. Brush tops with beaten egg and sprinkle with sugar. Bake at 400 for about 15 minutes. (This can also be made into braided loaves or baked in 3 loaf pans; allow about 10 more minutes baking time.)

Morry and Florence Ekstrand: "Lucia Buns." From *Notes From a Scandinavian Kitchen*. Welcome Press, 1980.

A Merrie Prairie Christmas

Christmases Present

The Northern Christmas

A Forum Editorial

Call us biased, but we think Christmas in the northern states is wonderful.

North Dakota, Minnesota and South Dakota are known for nasty winter weather, but during the holiday season cold and snow are assets to savor. After all, we live in one of the few places in the nation where that ideal "white Christmas" is almost a guarantee.

On this Christmas Eve day shoppers will be rushing to make those last-minute gift purchases and families will be gathering in homes across the region. Youngsters, their faces glowing from the frosty breeze, will enjoy thrilling sled rides down the snow-covered Red River dike. Later, churches will be filled with worshippers expressing in song and prayer the real meaning of the season. A traditional Christmas Eve dinner and maybe the opening of gifts are also on the agenda.

And what makes those things so special in northern latitudes? Only that the cold and snow and frosty windows contribute to the "feeling" of the season. Call it the Christmas spirit. Call it old-fashioned traditionalism. Call it the kind of corny idealism depicted in Currier and Ives prints. It's all of those things and more.

We don't mean to diminish Christmas in warm climates. But as northerners, the prospect of barbecuing ribs on a deck overlooking a warm ocean while the relatives smear sunscreen on their noses, is foreign to us. Somehow, the tropical breeze in the palm trees doesn't cut it for us at Christmas.

The warmth and spirit which will fill homes tonight display a uniquely northern characteristic: When it's cold and blustery outside, the holiday gatherings indoors seem warmer, closer, more filled with the aura of this extra- ordinary season. The wonder in children's eyes is deeper because they know Santa can land those reindeer and that sleigh in the snow. And the account of the Christ child's birth in a stable becomes even clearer as we understand He shivered — in the cold.

We understand, of course, that the meaning of Christmas transcends climate. The holiday observances of peoples in warm lands are no less valuable and legitimate than are the traditions of those of us who live in the north. Yet, we count ourselves among the very fortunate to live in North Dakota and Minnesota at Christmastide. The contrast of our frigid weather with the warm inner glow that comes with this season sharpens our appreciation of the holiday.

Merry Christmas.

Reprinted from *The Forum of Fargo-Moorhead*, Dec. 24, 1988.

Christmas As I Think It Used To Be

Jerome D. Lamb

It was the weather, not Christmas, Mark Twain said everyone talks about but no one does anything about. People do things about Christmas, so many things that stress and fatigue have become as prominent a part of the holiday landscape as candles sticks and pine cones. Besides, Mark Twain didn't have much to say about Christmas one way or the other. As I recall he pretty much ignored it, unlike Charles Dickens and Dylan Thomas and thousands and thousands of others, including me. Every December I unload a few hundred fresh words on the season, and a few months later, at re-reading time, see that I missed the mark again. And so I sigh, and, come next December, try again.

It probably started in whatever the year was when I first heard the voice of Dylan Thomas, rolling off the tight black valleys of the Caedmon record, winding "A Child's Christmas in Wales" about the room. Since then or before I've longed to do something literary about my Christmases: trap them with words, stuff them on paper, so that I at least, to say nothing of my children and grandchildren and even unwary strangers, will always know how splendid and wonderful those days were.

There are problems however. To start with I am not Dylan Thomas, and the prairie where all but one of my Christmases have taken place is not the two-tongued, sea-cornered, character-laden Welsh town of his memory. There were in my Christmases no gongs bombulating, no Mrs. Protheroes, no stalking cats, no port-loving aunts standing in the snow, singing like big-bosomed thrushes. There were uncles, but they were neither as numerous nor as ominous as the Thomas uncles. There were, most of the time, snow and church and large, perfect meals, eaten with the good silver. And socks and pajamas in abundance, and the sad knowledge, when the day was ending, that it would not come again for a whole year. Forever.

But there is nothing terribly unique about any of that; no firemen, no tigers skulking along the back fence, nor wolves, nor birds the color of red flannel petticoats. It seems to me that my childhood Christmases are lacking in specificity. One does not come across as much different than the next. I can vaguely recall Eddie Milligan in a red suit and an unconvincing beard passing out hard candy to us, the smaller people, at a school program. He looked much less authentic as Santa Claus than he did in the summertime when he was an Indian chief.

I remember another school program when I was nine and was obliged to appear in long underwear dyed black (leotards had not yet come to the prairie) and a short velvet dress-like thing, put on backwards. I was impersonating some sort of herald:

"Hew ye, Hew ye, most gwacious King,

All wise and just in evwything."

I am reported to have proclaimed. Erroneously I suspect; The fault must have been not in my enunciation but rather in the peculiar acoustics of that lunch-room-auditorium-sometime-chapel, now disappeared into the base of a hospital parking lot.

And I remember when I was eight my mother doused the plum pudding with heated brandy, preparatory to flaming the whole scrumptious mound, and I, total abstainer and pure creature that I was, refused to eat it, and my brother laughed at me, and tears came to my eyes, and my mother defended my right to be righteous. Afterwards I felt somewhat foolish, and abandoned abstinence.

But those are almost the only things I recall distinctly from my childhood Christmases; oh, every one was the best ever, I suppose, until I was about twelve and the years of socks and pajamas and long afternoons in which there was never anything to do set in. The next four or five were all right, but definitely not the best ever. And then I went away from home, and the memorable Christmases began.

Now, nearly forty years later, it seem that most of those splendid Christmases began in the great cavern of St. Paul's Union Depot, where my first year out I stumbled across my brother — the plum pudding brother — in the teeming throng. His was the first familiar face in three months; familiar too was the biting air and the curtains of steam we hustled through on the platform of the track where the Manitoba Flyer was then loading. And the dusty mothball smell of the ancient car we boarded was familiar, the stove in one corner, the dyspeptic brakeman in the other, and those wonderful benches, upholstered in the railroad's own patented and everlasting green mohair, with backs that could be flopped either way, allowing the traveler — when the car was not full — a spacious, leg-stretching journey into the night.

Oh, the night; the great moon and crisp stars, white fields at the black edge of the woods, and wheels click-clicking across Minnesota, past St. Cloud, Sauk Center, Alexandria, Fergus Falls, past barns and frozen lakes and pastures and sleeping towns. I propped my head on a rented pillow and looked out the window the whole night, and after thirty hours of wet, grey winter along the New York Central and the Boston and Maine I kept saying to myself "I'm home! I'm home!" My brother slept.

Home was never so much home as it was those dozen or fifteen years between the time I went away and the time I had my own, another home. Those are the years that stick in my memory, the years of talking 'til four in the morning, of sleeping late, of long dinners, of arguing for the sake of argument, pleased with our wit and the amazing discovery that all of us had, more or less, grown up a little. Years of fires in the fireplace, sprigs of pine artfully strewn about the odd shelves, and cellophane bells dangling from the loops of window shades. And on the dining table a patch of no-longer-snow-white cotton batting, in the midst of which sat a primitive sleigh and rather gaunt Siberian celluloid Santa in blue pants, his beard attached with a small snip of adhesive tape. A spikey tinsel rope wrapped around his shoulders linked him to four — or was it six? — cast metal elk, who looked a good deal more like the Hartford Insurance than Donner and Blitzen. The crown and horns of one had somehow become detached years back, and were now held on by rubber bands, but the illusion was not destroyed. Those were illusion-filled years, where the winter beyond the muslin tie-back curtains was always a clean and windless winter, except for the time we had a dust storm on Christmas Day, and another brother, freshly jilted, brooded beside a scraggly balsam tree. But that was towards the end of the great Christmases. We were marrying by then, our parents aging, the trains no longer running. Reality, like January, was coming on.

I know of course that it was never, even then, quite as wonderful as memory would have us believe; that sentimentality filters out the dirty dishes, the touchy feelings, the long trips back to drab dorms, dismal army camps, dingy office and classrooms, where the rest of the year lurked. We were, I know, neither as bright nor as happy as we supposed ourselves to be, nor were the winters as cozy as distance makes them seem. The past remembered is usually a better place than the past when it was present. And yet ... and yet those trains were real, those trips back home, those long nights with the fire blazing. The things were really there; the tree in the corner, the elk on the table, the plum pudding on the counter. And the people; changed or gone now, all of us, but we were there, alive and warm, and up to our foreheads in hope. Color them how we will, deck them out with boughs of imaginary holly, and set them in snow deeper and softer and whiter than any snow has ever been, those Christmases were real. And fine. And never quite forgotten.

Jerome D. Lamb: "Christmas As I Think It Used To Be." From *the small voice*, Fargo, North Dakota, 1984.

A Merrie Prairie Christmas

Windbreak: Winter

Linda Hasselstrom

December 24: *On a ranch near Hermosa, South Dakota: Low -35, high -15.*

I called Jim and Mavis and advised them not to come for Christmas. The entrance road is completely closed by huge drifts and the pasture route risky. But their pipes are frozen and they're sick of working on them, so they're coming anyway.

When we got to the corral this morning we found a cow down. We tried to get her on her feet but she was too far gone. She was lying with her head downhill, so I suppose her lungs filled with fluid. She looked so thin I checked her teeth, and found the bottom front ones worn nearly away. All the feed in the world wouldn't have helped her. We can't get through the drifts to the boneyard so tonight she's lying in the driveway looking very small and pitiful.

We are continuing to feed cake, hay, and alfalfa cubes to all the cattle, but they still seem weak and lacking in energy, as well as terribly footsore. The yearling calves look gaunt even though they're getting all the creep feed and alfalfa cubes they can eat. Too much will make them bloat.

Jim tried to come in the main road, got stuck and dug out without us seeing him, and then parked the truck half-way to the house in the pasture and walked the rest of the way. I heard Mavis yell, and opened the door in time to see her teetering through the drifts in high-heeled boots, shrieking, "Damn Christmas! To hell with living in the country!" We had a good visit around a supper of chili and cornbread, enhanced with scotch for the men, brandy for me and pink squirrels for Mavis, and played cards until late.

December 25, Christmas: *Low -25. high 10 above; feels like spring.*

I'm keeping Father's journal too, now. He always leaves it for me so he'll know later what the temperatures were during the winter. Naturally I read back through what he's written. Mostly he sticks to the facts: the work done, which cows are with the bulls, how much rain we get. But it will be a wonderful record to have in the years ahead; already he uses it to settle arguments with Harold about exactly how much rainfall we got in a certain year, or how much snow. Mother also keeps one, though I've never seen it. I'm pleased to know we're all recording life in our own ways, though I wish I had children to pass all these journals to.

We all went together to feed, and got Jim's truck in as far as the house at noon before stuffing ourselves on ham and turkey.

Mavis reminded me of the last time we were together on Christmas, a couple of years ago. It was the first nice day for awhile so we moved the cows home from over east. At the very last pasture gate I was shouting at George and Jim, who were riding in the pickup in front of the cattle while Mavis walked, and I rode, behind. My horse slipped on the ice and fell, with my right leg under her. My head hit the frozen ground and I was knocked cold.

When I came to, Jim, who has had EMT training, was checking to see if my legs were broken, and Mavis, a nurse, was looking at my pupils and saying I had a concussion. George loaded me in the pick-up and we headed for the house. After a minute I asked why Jim and Mavis were here.

George: "Because it's Christmas."

Linda: "Then why are we moving cattle?"

He laughed — said later it was the first sensible thing I'd said all day. I was dizzy the rest of the day — my second concussion from having a horse fall with me. Mother always said my real father's family was famous for having hard heads. Grandmother Bovard fell on her head in a bathtub once and knocked a chunk out of the tub.

December 26: *Low -30, high -5, with 50-mile-an-hour winds.*

Jim and Mavis went back to their frozen pipes. The folks called from Texas; they made it safely and are settling into their apartment, but someone had broken in and stolen their TV.

Started reading Loren Eiseley's *Star Thrower.* Ray Bradbury wrote at Eiseley's death that he "stepped down to lace his bones with ancient dogs and prairie shadows." May we all.

Auden said Eiseley was "a man unusually well trained in the habit of prayer, by which I mean the habit of listening. The petitionary aspect of prayer is its most trivial because it is involuntary."

I like that thought. I've long since given up asking the being we call God for anything, but I often think of HIm in appreciation — when enjoying the songs of the blackbirds, for example. I think He must be much more sensible than the Christians insist, and make allowances for people like me.

I remember my father, one Christmas eve when I was a child, asking my mother and me if we really believed that a child had been born in a manger to take the world's sins on himself. At the time, I believed it passionately, but I was uneasy about my father in relation to religion. Even then he never went to church, but I knew I couldn't respect a God who would condemn him to hell.

Linda Hasselstrom: "Windbreak: Winter." From *Windbreak.*
Barn Owl Books, 1987.

Christmas Lights

Cathy Mauk

Long ago, when fast food was the lunch counter at Woolworth's, when the mall was a cornfield and Herbst Department Store seemed destined for eternal merchant reign, our family launched a tradition. We'd go out to eat, a rare treat, and then we'd pile in the car and spend the evening driving up and down the streets of these two towns looking at Christmas lights.

I think we did.

We must have; I remember too clearly. Yet it seems almost impossible now, when time spent driving around town is usually time spent running late, when we've become accustomed to the sophistication of electronic scoreboards and computerized fireworks extravaganzas, that we would have enjoyed something as simple as houses strung with colored lights.

But we did. We must have, for I remember how one tradition evolved into another, and how our taste in lights reflected our ages and experiences.

As little children, my brother and I were most impressed by the houses that wore the most lights, believing, as do most children, that more is better. The houses with the most lights, or the most garish display of lights, always won our award. And if a house had both thousands of lights, preferably blinking lights, and a plywood Santa atop the roof — with loudspeakers blaring "Up on the Housetop" — the others didn't stand a chance.

As adolescents, we fancied ourselves arbiters of cool. We most liked those lighting displays with a touch of whimsy, or silliness, or impressive, avant garde design.

Too, it was in our adolescence that, with some encouragement from a parent whose sense of humor runs toward the absurd, we began selecting the winner of our very own award for tacky. This tradition became firmly entrenched in family history when we noticed that those displays that made us snicker often were named winners in the very real contest sponsored then by the Chambers of Commerce.

Because of our family lights-viewing tradition, I consider myself something of a fan, if not an expert, of Christmas lighting displays. Even in adulthood, even in a hurry as I drive down a Fargo street late for an appointment, I consider which of those houses would have been contender when we were kids.

As I grew older, my travels exposed me to exquisite Christmas lighting displays. I have seen the President of the United States light the national Christmas tree and the White House a-drip with Christmas splendor. I have seen 300-year-old tidewater Virginia mansions festooned with greenery, beeswax candles and tree ornaments of spun gold. I have seen an estate in Maryland with a room constructed for the display of the owner's village of miniature Victorian houses, each lit from within, each surrounded by sparkling artificial snow and the whole town circled by a gold-plated limited edition Lionel train.

There was a time when they impressed me.

Now I far prefer humbler displays. I like the displays of small towns, their one or two strands of lights swathed in faded green plastic garland, swaying in the wind over the near-empty streets. I like thinking that someone — maybe the local cop, maybe one of the few remaining merchants — hauled out the ladder and put up the lights that the city council bought in 1967. I like to think that when he hung the lights, he felt he was doing an important thing in making ready for Christmas.

I liked places like the Cash Town cafe and bus station in Ortonville, Minnesota, before it was recently remodeled. Then, it had cracked linoleum and tables that always rocked and the rips in the brittle gold plastic of the booths were sutured with duct tape. I like that they decorated for Christmas. On a wall behind a counter was a cardboard banner of cut-out letters spelling HAPPY HOLIDAYS. The green and red had faded to lime green and pink and the second P hung out of kilter, but you got the message. On the serve-yourself coffee table, near the two-burner Bunn coffee maker and the plastic wrapped slices of pie and the glass canister of doughnuts was a two-foot Christmas tree made of pipe cleaners and graced with little pink balls so old that half their paint had rubbed off to expose swatches of silver. It was the warmest sight I saw that cold day.

Now, I prefer the single electric candles hung in the windows of dilapidated houses, or the lights of an artificial tree twinkling from an attic apartment.

For it's the dingy little house that dares celebrate Christmas that reveals the holiday's message. It's the grubby little cafe and bus station that most needs to greet travelers with the Christmas promise of hope and grace. It's the empty streets of small valley towns that, lit by the single string of old Christmas lights, most need something in which to rejoice.

It's the light amid the commonplace and the ordinary that can make even an adult think perhaps there's a Christmas after all.

Cathy Mauk: "Christmas Lights." From *The Forum of Fargo-Moorhead*, Dec. 24, 1988.

A Merrie Prairie Christmas

But Baby It's Cold Outside: Memories of Minnesota Winters

Craig Hergert

> *Winter is icummen in,*
> *Leyden's sing Goddamm,*
> *Raineth drop and staineth slop,*
> *And how the wind doth ramm!*
> *Lhude sing: Goddamm.*
> *– Ezra Pound: "Ancient Music."*

According to the Encyclopedia Britannica, the name for winter comes from an old Germanic word meaning "time of water." Leave it to the Germans to goof up a name. The folks who should have been charged with naming the season between fall and spring are the Minnesotans. Minnesotans learn about winter the old-fashioned way: They survive it. I have survived twenty-four Minnesota winters, and I think two dozen is quite enough, so for the past four years I've been wintering in Ohio. You can't really call Ohio's post-fall/pre-spring season *winter*. To be accurate, you'd have to call it a winter sampler. You find out what winter is like in Ohio, but you really don't experience a whole one. In Minnesota, however, a person can experience the real thing.

> *If winter comes, can spring be far behind?*
> *– Percy Byshe Shelley: "Ode to the West Wind"*

If Shelley had asked that question in Minnesota, he would have been laughed out of the state. Spring can be and is far behind winter in Minnesota. Forget about that December 22 to March 21 nonsense. In Minnesota winter officially begins after the World Series and ends, God willing, some time in April. The two worst winters I lived through were in 1968, when I was twelve years old, and 1982, when I had lived through enough cold weather to think I didn't mind it. I was wrong. I still minded it plenty. During the winter of '81-'82, Minneapolis, where I lived at the time, got ninety-nine inches of snow. *Ninety-nine inches.* When I first heard that, I was rooting for one more inch so that we could boast about hitting the century mark, but the truth is I didn't want one more inch. I didn't want one more flake. Ever again.

Even worse than the amount of snow that winter, was the wind chill. Minnesotans are obsessed with wind chill in the winter the way

Ohioans are with humidity in the summer. "It's not the heat, it's the humidity," we'll explain to out-of-state visitors who stand sweltering before us, not caring what the exact cause of their discomfort is. Wind chill refers to what the temperature feels like because of a good, stiff Northern wind regardless of what the bank thermometer says the temperature is. When I was home for Christmas break in December of '83, the temperature one night was twenty below, which, as a native Minnesotan, I laugh at — if, that is, my long-johns are on and the furnace is running. The wind I'dchill, though, was *ninety below zero*. I don't laugh at those numbers, even as a native Minnesotan.

My earliest winter memory is from when I was about five years old. My two-year-old sister, Kristi, and I were all bundled up and playing in the backyard. I have no idea what we could have been doing that would have been considered playing since I remember being awfully cold, but Mom said, "Go out and play," so we went out and moved around and figured that would satisfy her. Although my memory of this event is sketchy, I know that something went wrong. Kristi got hurt or upset or something and wanted me to take her back in. As I headed her for the steps of the house, I remember seeing the tears on her cheek turn to ice. When I saw that happen, I got her in the house *real* fast. For all I knew, other parts of her — or of me, for that matter — were going to be next.

I should probably quit telling that; most of my specific memories of winter are positive. The negative ones, even the ones from the most severe winters, seem to have all melted together like a pile of April slush. The positive memories, meanwhile, remain as distinct as a snowflake.

The most joyous part of winter for a kid was school closings. I remember the night I saw my first episode of *Hawaii Five-O*. My parents were down the block at a friend's house, and there was a genuine Minnesota blizzard raging outside the picture window. My older sister, Sandy, a veteran of four more winters than I, made her prediction: "There's no way there's going to be school tomorrow." Few words ever sounded as beautiful to a twelve-year-old who hadn't yet finished the next day's fraction problems. We stayed up until ten — unheard of at the time — and I watched in wonder as, ten feet from the window and the storm, McGarret and Danno ran around Hawaii in short sleeves.

School closings were a special occasion, not just for me but for my whole family. They meant that my dad, a sixth-grade English teacher, would be around for the whole day. And they meant that we would have potato pancakes with the elementary school principal. I have no idea how this family tradition started. On the morning of a school closing, Dad would call Paul Olson, the principal, and invite him over for a potato pancake lunch. Mr. Olson would accept, and Mom would spend the next hour converting a bag of potatoes into mounds of shreds. Mr. Olson, a small man with a surprisingly explosive laugh, would arrive around 11:30 and sit in the dining room talking to Dad while my sisters and I were in the living room, watching the game shows that school normally denied us. Meanwhile, Mom was in the kitchen frying four potato pancakes at a time and bringing them out to the dining room as fast as they were ready. To me, potato pancakes with apple sauce and Paul Olson's laughter on the side were as much a part of winter as overshoes and parkas.

My fondest school closing, though, happened in the spring of 1968. The night before, there had been a freezing rain and by morning the roads were completely frozen over. Since it would have been dangerous for the buses to be out, school was closed. But around ten o'clock something wonderful happened: Spring arrived on that very day. With the sun shining and the temperatures mild, I ran outside to cash in on this free day of recreation and saw something I'll never forget. Because the streets were still covered with ice, there were no cars out, but there were kids out. Kids, a half dozen of them, from the other side of town were ice-skating on the street. It was like watching a pint-sized version of the Ice Capades.

> In seed time learn, in harvest teach, in winter enjoy.
> — William Blake: "Proverbs of Hell."

Those kids who skated on the street were merely responding to an instinct all Minnesotans have — the instinct to not only survive winter, but to conquer it. The cold doesn't keep kids indoors. When Mother asks, "Don't you want to go out and play?" the kid wouldn't think of saying "Are you kidding? In that cold?" The kid is out. The kid can handle the big chill. I expressed that instinct a little differently than most Northerners. Most of the kids could skate, and so they spent as much time as they could out on the town skating rink. Not me. I had skates, of course. Not to have skates would have been as unnatural as not having feet. So when I was ten, my parents bought me a pair of brown ones with thick, imposing blades. My ankles, though, refused to cooperate. They would both collapse, simultaneously, so that the blades were no longer on the ice but parallel to it, and my legs, following my ankles' lead, fanned out like Jerry Lewis's. Scott Hamilton I wasn't. But a Minnesotan I was, and so I still was attracted to the ice. Despite giving up on skates when I was ten, I played hockey when I was thirteen. As I recall I was the only hockey player who wore boots. Wayne Gretzky I wasn't either.

What I did enjoy was ice fishing, a winter sport which has more to do with winter than sport and more to do with ice than fishing. When I was fifteen and singing in the church choir, Earl Devins, a middle-aged basso profundo, adopted me as his ice fishing partner. Sundays after church he'd pick me up, outfit me with a snowmobile suit and fishing boots, and take me to Lake Shetek where we would stand in the middle of the lake for five or six hours, usually without the benefit of a fish house. Earl would drill a hole in the ice with a hand auger while I watched. For me, a scrawny fifteen-year-old, to have handled the task would have meant the loss of an hour's fishing time. It took Earl only ten grueling minutes. The hole drilled, we could fish, sort of. Winter turns every aspect of fishing into a challenge — hooking a minnow, unhooking a fish, and, especially, waiting in between the two.

Usually we wouldn't catch more than a dozen perch and after a couple of hours on the surface of the lake, they looked the way I felt, coated by a thin layer of ice. Once in a while, though, we caught something more, and that would keep us heading back, Sunday after Sunday. I remember one time when, my patience wearing thin, I had just about decided to sit in the car for awhile to warm up. Just then my bobber, barely visible since the sun had gone down a couple of hours ago, sank like a stone. Grabbing my sawed-off fishing pole, I was ice-fisherman enough to know that this was no perch. Seeing my commotion, Earl came over to help. After a few minutes of struggle, we pulled it out of the ice — a five-pound northern pike. I was so proud I didn't notice what Earl noticed immediately. The northern was wrapped up in my line, but wasn't attached to my hook. It was attached to Earl's. We decided to chalk it up as an interception.

Earl and I had one more outing that winter, no northerns this time, just the dozen medium-sized perch. Then spring came, as it finally does, even in Minnesota, and we had to put away the ice fishing gear. But we didn't put the gear far away. In Minnesota, if spring comes, can winter really be far behind?

Craig Hergert: "But Baby It's Cold Outside: Memories of Minnesota Winters." Reprinted with permission from *From the Heartlands.* Bottom Dog Press, 1988.

A Merrie Prairie Christmas

Christmas in the Kitchen

Coins of the Realm

Susan Hauser

New snow today. How I love to watch it fall. It lazes down from the sky, the way I would like to move through my life, taking my time, and riding a little now and then on a warm updraft that passes by.

Gradually and thoroughly, it covers the ground, at first filling up all the tiny spaces between the browned grass blades, then moving up to surround fallen leaves. Finally it overcomes the twigs and branches blown down by the last dry wind. By tomorrow it will *be* the ground and we will measure the winter by its depth.

Now that the scenery is right, I can begin to think more seriously about Christmas. It is the last obstacle to the fine silence and solitude of mid-winter. In an intense two weeks of glorification, gifting and gregariousness, we will fill ourselves with the company of others. And when the door of December closes and leaves us locked in the new year, we will, like animals fattened for hibernation, be able to live off the accumulated chaos and good feelings for a good eight to ten weeks.

As every bear and chipmunk knows, the gluttony necessary to a safe passage through the dark caves of January and February requires dedicated preparation. We have enough instinct left to understand that and, being closer to our nature than we readily admit, food becomes the focus of our campaign to consort with our species.

Cookies are the touchstone for me: icons of Christmases past. Their making was itself part of the festival. For a week my sisters and brothers and mother and I gathered in the kitchen after dinner and worked dough. Each night was devoted to a different kind of cookie. For Russian tea cakes we stood at the table and rolled little balls of dough in our hands. Then, after baking, we rolled them in powdered sugar, then rolled them in powdered sugar again. Spritz were the easiest, and caused the most trouble. We fought over the cookie press...at first for the right to use it, then for the right to rest our broken fingers.

Rosettes were the scariest. We took turns standing on a chair in front of the stove, dipping the long stemmed iron butterfly into batter and then into a sinister kettle of simmering oil. Sugar cookies were the hardest...because they took the longest: rolling, baking, cooling, decorating. By the time the last silver bead blessed the top of the last Christmas tree, everyone was ready for cool air and solitude.

We found both out on the lake, on the black disc of ice that we kept clear of snow. We pushed ourselves around in little circles, not talking, not touching. Sometimes far out where the water is deep, the ice would crack. The sound exploded in the dark and echoed across the waste of snow, making us glad for the light from the house.

We never stayed out long. The cookies still had some power over us, and when the ice yelped a second time, we let ourselves be drawn back to the kitchen, where we sneaked one last handful of our favorites and went our separate ways.

However much the initial pleasure gave way to the pain of an over-done passion, the cookies paid off. Coins of the realm when company came by, they bought a spontaneous chorale of oohs and ahs from grown-ups who remembered. Children liked them, too, because they tasted so good. And there were enough to last right through to New Year's Day, when no one wanted to cook any more. In fact, no one wanted to even talk to anybody else.

In my memory, it was always a bright, bright day. The sun shone hard on the snow. The wind had come the night before and stolen our tracks from the lake. Nobody called on the phone. There was nothing much to watch on TV. One at a time, we would rummage through the ravaged cookie tins and boxes, cleaning out the last broken pieces of the holidays. I took my share back to my room, closed the door, and let myself down into the pages of a new book. When I came out again, it would be spring.

Susan Hauser: "Coins of the Realm." From *Meant To Be Read Out Loud*. Loonfeather Press: 1988.

Russian Tea Cakes

Good any time of year!

> 1 cup soft margarine or butter
> 1/2 cup powdered sugar
> 1 tsp. vanilla
> 2 1/4 cups flour
> 1/4 tsp. salt
> 3/4 cup chopped walnuts

Cream first three ingredients. Stir in remaining ingredients. Chill dough. Roll into balls about 1 inch in diameter. Bake on greased cookie sheet at 400 degrees for 10-12 minutes. Roll immediately in powdered sugar. When cool, roll in powdered sugar again.

Yield: four dozen

Susan Hauser

A Merrie Prairie Christmas

Remembering Gram

Andrea Hunter Halgrimson

My grandma was an extraordinary woman. She's often on my mind. I see her kindness, gentleness and love reflected in my mother's ways. Christmas and Gram's December birthday intensify the memory of her presence.

Grandma loved Christmas. Images of her clothed in a calico apron trimmed in colored bias tape come and go this time of year.

Her hair is wound on top of her head in a grandmotherly bun. Wisps of grey fly out around her face. Her hands, grown knotty at the knuckles, are mixing dough.

She's baking cookies for the holiday celebration.

In the early 1900s, as a young girl, Grandma left her home in Norway and sailed to America to avoid an unwanted marriage. Betrothed by her father, as was the custom then, to a man she did not want to marry, she escaped with her mother's help, certainly not the custom then.

Grandma landed at Ellis Island and came by rail to North Dakota, a trip familiar to thousands of immigrants. My father (her son-in-law) told a story about Grandma's train ride.

Never having seen a banana, she chose one from the lunch cart. Daddy teased her, saying Gram ate the banana skin and all. Grandma always denied it saying she waited to see what others did.

Gram travelled to Lisbon, North Dakota, where her mother's sister lived. Her first job was as a cook. She lived and cooked in a wooden trailer. Called a cook car, it was hauled from farm to farm to provide workers' meals. She also worked as a domestic.

Poor treatment by her employers convinced her to seek an education and in 1910 she graduated from St. Luke's School of Nursing, Fargo. Eventually she married the brother of a classmate and they moved to Dazey, North Dakota. Her husband died shortly after her daughter's birth. When my mother was twelve, they moved back to Fargo and Gram returned to her career as a nurse.

She retired from nursing and came to live with us when my two younger brothers and I were children. She cared for all of us, my parents too, until she died.

Grandma had been visiting a friend in Minneapolis when she got sick. It was early in December. Mom and I drove down to bring her home.

The next day she went to the hospital for tests. When she came home we knew she wouldn't live much longer.

We celebrated her eighty-second birthday and shortly thereafter Gram got out her aprons and started baking for Christmas.

She baked day after day, preparing all of our family's traditional holiday cookies, my mother at her side. They stood for hours by the stove pouring batter on the krumkaker iron, cooking them and shaping them on a wooden cone. The recipe, shared by our neighbor to the north, makes a batch of eight dozen.

Neat rows of gold krumkaker cones were placed in a heavy cardboard coat box (the container of choice for years) and carried to the fruit room in the cool basement beneath our old house. The cookies were safe from yearning children afraid of gremlins we imagined lurking in the darkened cellar.

The krumkaker were soon joined by smaller boxes of spritz gently squeezed from the spritzer in zig-zag shapes crisply ridged after baking.

Buttery berlinakranse dough was rolled into pieces half again as long as a little finger and tied in a knot. At the knot's intersection, a dab of egg white was applied serving as glue to attach a sparkling scrap of loaf sugar.

Sandbakkels were the most difficult to make but because of that offered the most mistakes — for tasting. Each ball of almond-flavored dough was pressed into a tin, baked, and if one was lucky, removed in one piece. Embossed with the tin's pattern, the cookies looked like sculptured shells.

I think one of the things that sustained Gram was knowing that her favorite grandchild would be back for Christmas. My older brother was working in the Caribbean as a sailor. My husband had located him with a newspaper ad and sent him a ticket to fly home.

With the baking done, the celebrating began. Friends came calling, my brother came home and Gram made the pineapple krumkaker filling he loved. Mom and I prepared company dinners and family meals. Gram's old friend from Minneapolis arrived. It was a glorious time.

For years Grandma had been putting some of her small pension into a savings account "for the kids' inheritance." She wouldn't touch the money for any reason.

On Christmas Eve my brothers and I opened our present from Gram. Each of us received a check with a note saying she wanted to see us enjoy "our inheritance."

That special Christmas was twenty-one years ago. She died on February 4, 1968.

Our family, and those who knew my grandmother are still enjoying her inheritance of kindness and compassion, sharing and gentleness and love, the very things this holiday is all about.

The following recipes for krumkaker and pineapple filling came to my family from our neighbor Marg Scott. They are passed on with her permission.

I've added a few sentences of instructions to the method, but the recipe assumes that a grandma, mom or neighbor will show you how.

Krumkaker
9 eggs
1 pound sugar
1 pound butter
1 pound flour
1 cup water
3 tablespoons brandy
1 teaspoon powdered cardamom
1/2 teaspoon cinnamon
1/2 teaspoon vanilla

1. Beat eggs and sugar for 1 hour (15 minutes with electric beater). Melt butter and add to above mixture. Add water, spices and flour to above mixture. Beat all together until smooth.

2. Use about 1 tablespoon of batter at a time. Have iron hot. Cook until golden, turning iron as necessary. Remove krumkaker and shape on wooden cone while still hot. Leave on cone, seam side down until cooled. Add cold water to batter when it thickens. Makes about 8 dozen. (Recipe may be halved.)

Pineapple filling for krumkaker:
1 tablespoon gelatin
2 tablespoons cold water
1 cup scalded milk
1/2 cup sugar
1 cup canned crushed pineapple, drained
1 cup heavy cream

1. Soak gelatin in water for 5 minutes. Dissolve mixture in hot milk. Add sugar and stir to dissolve sugar.

2. Set bowl in cold water. Stir occasionally until mixture begins to thicken. Add pineapple and let stand until it begins to set. Fold in stiffly beaten cream and chill.

The next recipes are from my mother's recipe box. Some are in Grandma's handwriting. I don't know their origins except one came from Lena and another from Ruth. Methods and cooking times are sketchy or nonexistent. Again, assumptions are made about the cook's expertise. Common sense helps, too. I've used my grandma's spelling for the cookies' names.

Lena's Sprits

1 cup butter
1 cup sugar (scant)
2 eggs
Almond extract
2 1/4 cup flour, measured before sifting
Bake in 375 degree oven for 10 minutes. Good.

Sandbakkels

1 cup sugar
1 cup butter
2 1/2 cups flour, sifted
1 egg
1/2 cup finely chopped almonds, do not use meat grinder)
Cream butter and sugar. Then add egg and gradually add flour, mixing well. Add nuts last. Press dough into tins and bake at 325 to 350 degrees until evenly brown (about 10 minutes). Allow cookies to cool before attempting to remove them from tins.

Ruth's Berlinakranse

2 cups butter (cream it)
1 1/2 cups powdered sugar
Yolks of three hard-boiled eggs put through a sieve into the creamed butter and powdered sugar
3 raw egg yolks dropped into above batter and mixed
1 1/2 teaspoons almond extract
5 cups flour
Roll out into three long rolls. Cut off about size of pieces of fudge and shape. Dip in egg white and then in crushed loaf sugar.

Andrea Hunter Halgrimson: "Remembering Grandma." *The Forum of Fargo-Moorhead*, Dec. 21, 1988.

A Merrie Prairie Christmas

The Legend of the Christmas Rose

Florence Ekstrand

Not so well known as some of the Christmas stories and legends is that of the Christmas rose. But you will find the flower in Scandinavian needlework, often in exquisite cross stitch. The Christmas rose is white.

In a long ago time, Sweden banished its outlaws to a primitive forest region where they lived out their sentence, often with wife and children. One of these wives boasted to the local abbot how every year at Christmas, Goinge forest was transformed into a beautiful garden to commemorate the hour of Christ's birth. She was finally persuaded to lead the abbot, together with a lay brother, into the deep and craggy wilderness.

As they waited that night of Christmas Eve in the robber's cave, a strange illumination began to spread over the forest. The trees budded, the birds began to sing, flowers burst into bloom and berries formed on bushes, the fox and rabbit paraded their young.

The abbot was in a state of delight, trying to find the loveliest flower to bring to his archbishop. For the archbishop had promised pardon for the robber family if the abbot could produce just one flower from the promised spectacle.

But suddenly the lay brother could contain himself no longer. Surely all this, revealed as it was to these evil-doers, must not be of God but of the Devil. When a dove lighted on his shoulder he shouted, "Go thou back to hell from whence thou came!"

In an instant the scene began to fade and slowly disappeared. And the abbot lay dead on the snow. Clutched in his hand was a pair of white root bulbs, nothing more.

The lay brother planted them in the cloister but nothing came up and they were forgotten. But when Christmas Eve came round, green leaves pushed through the snow, crowned by silvery white petals. Overcome with awe, the brother took the flowers to the archbishop. True to his promise, he pardoned the robber.

Goinge forest never bloomed again. But the Christmas rose remains as a memory and a reminder that even to the least deserving of all the Christ reveals himself.

Once when I had baked rosettes at Christmas time, an elderly Norwegian lady chided me gently for dipping them in granulated sugar. "They should have just a dusting of powdered sugar over them," she told me. "It is the snow on the Christmas rose."

Florence Ekstrand: "Legend of the Christmas Rose." From *Notes From a Scandinavian Parlor*. Welcome Press: 1984.

The Ranch Woman's Guide To Christmas Cooking

Gwen Petersen

A treatise on getting ready and set for Thanksgiving and Christmas food consumption: Wherein one learns to be grateful for all that stuff one canned and froze. One also learns how to shortcut and come out smelling like a gourmet.

The calves have been sold, the weaner pigs have been sold, the land payment has been made and the human offspring are settled into the routine of school. The weather has held nicely. Really foul storms have not yet descended. Number one son has actually done his homework several times without being reminded. Grab all the bits of peace while you can because the Holidays are coming.

The Good Ranch Woman is required to bake, cook and create vast amounts of foods forever. It's a bad mark on your Ranch Woman's Merit Page if you go out to a restaurant for a holiday dinner or have anything catered or patronize a delicatessen. Since the last two aren't available in the country anyway, you have only the first item as an alternate choice to cooking. Even that my be taken from you since restaurants in country towns are apt to close during the holidays.

Organization and stamina are the keys to success. During this season of the year, try to avoid colds and flu. Even if you catch something, you are not allowed to take time out to be sick. Over the years, a thinking Ranch Woman will evolve an attack plan to cope with holidays. Some women develop a serious lassitude and have to be sent to a rest camp in Arizona. However, you are not financially prepared for that. And since the family won't pay attention to your symptoms anyway, you may as well roll up your sleeves.

Begin by dividing the work and activities into manageable segments. Segment one is food. You will need Thanksgiving food, Christmas food, New Year's food, and fancy tidbits for drop-in company, such as cute cookies and little stuffed pastry things.

First, pick a week around the middle of November. On day one, descend to the basement or tromp out to the root cellar taking along a big basket or box. Fill it with an assortment of canned fruits (especially apples), vegetables, and anything pickled. Back in the kitchen, search out the grinder, the chopping board, and the bread board. Have plenty of flour and sugar on hand.

In the freezer you have turkey, chicken and roasts you've been saving back. These present no problem besides drudgery. It's on the wide variety of fattening foods you must concentrate. Prepare a basic group of fancy breads, cakes and cookies. Think in terms of six batches of everything.

Stir up batter for six loaves each of two kinds of easy quick breads, such as carrot or applesauce. Add to each of these, raisins and smashed nuts. When the mixture tastes pretty good, pour it in loaf pans and stick in oven to bake. Always bake at a slow temperature. When still hot from the oven, pour on a lemon glaze. After the loaves cool, wrap individually in foil and freeze. That's one day's effort, and you are a little smug.

On day two, stir up a basic white cake and a basic spice applesauce cake recipe. It's best to double these recipes three times. Trying to stir up a six-times batter won't work. You don't have a big enough bowl unless you use the canner tub which you might not be able to lift to pour out the batter. To each of the cake recipes, add a lot of raisins, currants, dried fruits and some of those mashed nuts. Then add a half cup of liquor — any kind. Bake in loaf pans (fill only half full) at moderate temperature for a long time. Just before you stuff them in the oven, arrange maraschino cherry halves in artful designs over the tops.

These "fruitcakes" can be frozen when done 'til you are ready for them. Or they may be wrapped in cheese-cloth soaked in booze and placed in airtight containers. Three pound coffee cans are good. When you think about it, moisten the cheesecloth from time to time with brandy or some other liquor.

When the time comes, the fruitcakes can be served with a rum or brandy whipped cream. If you don't have the real rum or brandy, use vodka or gin with rum or brandy flavoring in it. No one can tell the difference. Be modest, be evasive when people exclaim over your superb fruitcakes and beg for the recipes. Mention (reverently) a pioneer ancestor who passed on the recipe with her dying breath while fighting off the hostiles. Baking the cakes along with all that tradition will have used up another day.

On the third day, stir up a big batch of yeast bread dough. Use buttermilk and several eggs in batter. After the dough has raised and you are ready to work it, do anything except make plain old loaves. Work out a variety of shapes. Spread the surfaces liberally with butter, sprinkle generously with cinnamon, raisins, currants and some more of those nuts. Leave some plain and some with just celery seed sprinkled over. Then roll, twist, fold or sandwich the shapes together and automatically you have five or six kinds of dinner rolls. Arrange these in foil pans and freeze. When needed, put them on the heater to raise, then bake when ready. After baking, frost some with interesting colors of frosting for "sweet rolls." Making the rolls requires another day. By this time, you may find your enthusiasm waning.

Cookie baking and tidbit fixing could take up the rest of the week. You are a fortunate woman if you love to bake cookies and little candy things. In which case, leave this to last and best. However, if by this time you're sick of the whole business, it's time to cash those cream checks you've been saving. Then call the lovely Norwegian lady who does specialty baking as a hobby. Order six dozen of everything she makes. There is, however, no need to chatter on to anyone about this.

Merely mark off day four on your calendar. That afternoon sit down and read from two to four p.m.[1]

On the fifth day, devote yourself to making jellies. You have lots of canned berry juice in the root cellar. All year you saved and collected small jars of assorted shapes, especially "cute" ones. Baby food jars are excellent if you are going through that stage. (Somebody in the area will be!) Make as many different varieties of jelly as you have kinds of juice. Do one recipe batch from each type of juice. (You'll have odd amounts of different flavors left over.) Fill the jars with the jelly and don't worry about more of one kind than another. Eventually you wind up with five or six varieties of teeny jars of jelly. Seal with paraffin and mark the name of each on one of those Christmasy Santa or angel stickers and paste it on the appropriate jelly. Lastly, spray paint all the jar lids a bright color.

Jelly making day is a tough day, but when finished, you have all those containers of actual homemade jelly to give away to people who stop by at Christmas.[2] Package them in variety packs and send to city friends who have everything. Take some to the Woman's Club "bring a gift" Christmas program.

Combine all the leftover bits of juice mentioned previously into one pot. Using a standard cup of sugar to a cup of juice recipe, make a final big batch of jelly and pour into large jars for the family and label "Fruit Surprise."

On the sixth day of what has shaped up to be a very long week, make candy. Some women are candy making experts. They have secret recipes handed down by the original candy witch. These ladies go to marvelous lengths to produce creams, mints, bonbons and un-named confections of all sorts. However, if candy making is not your bag, it works best to follow the recipe for fudge on the side of the cocoa box. Use real cream instead of milk and stir in a lot of extra butter and you can rarely miss. Think in terms of four. Make four

---

[1]Do not be tempted away from your reading program by housework or any emergency short of broken bones.

[2]City people always remark, "You MADE these YOURSELF!? When did you find time?"

batches of fudge, two plain and two with nuts. Prepare ahead several platters, plates and pie-pans heavily buttered and layered with Rice Crispies. Use two batches of fudge over the Rice Crispies. Spread the last two batches into plates or pans. Sprinkle the tops thickly with peanuts and/or coconut. (This is especially good for those people who like to pick nuts out of candy.) Always buy a jar of maraschino cherry halves at Christmas. On some the candy pieces, poke a half cherry for that professional touch.

If you feel you need another color of candy besides basic brown, make a penuche and do all the previously mentioned variations or make up some of your own.

An assortment of candy spread on a paper doily on a pseudo crystal serving dish looks terribly posh, especially if you add some of those Norwegian tidbits you ordered on day four. WARNING: Do not — under any circumstances — leave unprotected a confectionery arrangement, especially if you're planning it for company. Children, cats, dogs and husbands become notoriously untrustworthy in the face of such temptation. It's best to hide the dish. Take care no one is watching when you stash the treasure.

On the seventh day — rest!

Gwen Petersen: "The Ranch Woman's Christmas Cooking Guide." From *The Ranch Woman's Manual*, published by North Plains Press, Aberdeen, South Dakota, 1977.

Land of Lefse

Sylvia Paine

One of my favorite lunches is a peanut-butter-and-lefse sandwich. Lefse's subtlety makes it a perfect backdrop for the heartily assertive spread. The secret to a really good peanut-butter-and-lefse sandwich, however, isn't the main ingredients but butter. Without butter — lots of it — both the peanut butter and the lefse stick to the roof of your mouth.

To some, this shared trait is reason not to eat peanut butter or lefse. If you agree, you may have been prejudiced by dry commercial lefse, which has been compared to shoe leather. There is no other kind, you say? Not true.

It is possible to buy ethnically pure lefse, made without preservatives, and with real potatoes rather than dried-potato flakes. It is round and floppy and nicely freckled in a way that suggests it is baked and turned by hand, which it is. Not that it is old-fashioned lefse in the strict sense; the package label suggests the lefse be "warmed in microwave— use full power for five to ten seconds."

Although the lefse industry has not commissioned any surveys to prove it, the Twin Cities (thanks to our Scandinavian heritage) may well be the only metropolitan area in the nation where lefse is available in grocery stores year 'round, and Minnesota the only state where it is manufactured year 'round. Recipes for the flatbread, made simply of potatoes, flour, shortening and salt, came with our Scandinavian ancestors; today it is probably more popular here than in the Old Country. Our hunger for it is tremendous, says Merlin Hoiness, 71, who with his grandmother's recipe started what has become the state's premier lefse factory, Norsland Kitchens, now located in Rushford, about forty-five miles southeast of Rochester, where the landscape of woods, hills and rills recalls parts of Norway.

Hoiness was a grocer in nearby Harmony. "We never could buy enough lefse at the store to satisfy our customers," he says. "We had to buy from local people who were making it in their kitchens, which was illegal (because of the state health regulations). It was kind of like bootleg lefse. And if the inspector happened to find it, that was the end of that."

Now the factory sends one thousand packages of legal lefse all over the country each week through grocery distributors and mail order. "We've had trouble making it. The market is there."

The problem is twofold: Lefse is a labor-intensive product, and lefse dough tends to fall apart. When Hoiness started the business there was no equipment to speed production. Calls to New York City looking for lefse machinery proved futile and difficult to explain. Workers rolled dough by hand.

"I could run the lefse through a tortilla machine if I wanted to use what they call a dough stretcher, but it's strictly a preservative," Hoiness says. "It comes in pill form. I'm not interested in doing that."

Eventually he came up with a system that works like this: The potato-rich dough undergoes a preliminary flattening through something that works like an old washing-machine wringer. The dough is cut into rounds, which move along a conveyor belt until a worker hangs each piece over a hardwood lefse stick and flops it onto a lefse roller. These Rube Goldberg machines, which Hoiness invented, consist of a motor, a marble lazy susan that gives the lefse a quarter turn at regular intervals, and a roller that jumps on the round of dough like a wrester coming off the ropes, flattens it and lifts up for the next attack — twenty-five times in all. The machines make a tremendous racket and hops around from all the action. When it's nicely thin, the lefse is lifted onto a hot gas griddle, baked and turned and placed on another conveyor belt, to be delivered to someone who folds each round by hand and vacuum-seals two in a package.

A fine dusting of flour covers surfaces and people after a few minutes in the factory. The scent of baking lefse recalls wonderful memories of standing over a griddle, waiting for my mother to hand me a warm piece to butter and savor.

Our hurried, harried lives lack continuity. Eating lefse restores some sense of tradition. This, I believe, more than its taste, explains why Minnesotans eat so much lefse.

"Lefse is part of Minnesota," Joyce Wahlquist says, her voice ringing with conviction over the phone from Starbuck, home of the world's largest lefse. "People take their lefse quite seriously. It isn't a joking matter."

In 1983 as part of the town's centennial, folks in Starbuck made a lefse of nine feet, eight inches in diameter. Two trial runs produced mixed results: One succeeded, one failed miserably when the dough "just didn't hang together," Wahlquist says. On the big day, with hundreds of people watching, the lefse crew rolled the dough with a giant makeshift rolling pin and lifted it over to the grill — steel sheets set on railroad ties over a charcoal fire. A roar of celebration went up as it landed safely. It was baked, measured, cut, buttered and handed out. "It wasn't the world's *greatest* lefse, but they ate it all up," Wahlquist says.

Years from now we will look back and recognize this time as one of transition for lefse. Fifty years ago, lefse was lefse; today, it must be explained, usually by comparison with tortillas, even in places like Rushford, where a restaurant with "Velkommen" rosemaled on its wall routinely serves taco salad and egg rolls but not lefse.

And who learns to make lefse anymore? "The older generation is passing on and the younger ones are not picking it up," Hoiness says, "but being raised on it they're anxious to eat lefse again." Around Minnesota lefse factories are springing up: in Lake Park and Gonnvick, Hitterdal, and Hawley.

Last fall — "prime lefse season," says Stuart Bell, co-owner of Trudeau Distributing in Eagan, which trucks Norsland lefse and one other brand to about one hundred twenty-five stores in Minnesota, — "we couldn't come close to supplying the demand. We probably received only a quarter of the lefse we could have sold."

The challenge for the burgeoning lefse industry lies in convincing non-Scandinavians to eat their product. But unlike tortillas, which have been universally embraced, lefse has an image problem. Hoiness knows, because when he gives lefse demonstrations here and there, "inevitably people will come up and say, 'Oh, that lutefisk stuff.' They mix up lefse with lutefisk — they can't remember the difference."

To that end he is publishing a book featuring ninety-one ways to use lefse: as pizza crust, as a taco shell, layered with fillings and cut bite-size as an hors d'oeuvre, filled with meat like a sandwich or fruit like a crepe, even rolled up with beans and lettuce and hot sauce as a substitute for tortillas. There is no end of things to put on it or in it. "Face it," Hoiness says: "Lefse by itself is bland."

Sylvia Paine: "Land of Lefse." From *Mpls/St. Paul* Magazine, December 1988.

A Merrie Prairie Christmas

Christmas on the Lighter Side

Mom, I Hate To Tell You This, But....

Nancy Edmonds Hanson

Mother, I'm sorry to have to finally tell you, but perhaps it's best this way.

Yes, I know. I know the truth. The spirit of Santa Claus may live in all of us (as Francis Church of the *New York Sun* wrote to little Virginia so many years ago), but it's you — you! — who's been responsible for three decades of walnuts, bubble bath and rock-hard red-and-green ribbon candy.

I've kept mum for, oh, the last several dozen of my holiday seasons because I didn't want to spoil Christmas for you and Dad. You seemed to be having so much fun. I let you continue to set the alarm for 5 a.m. so you could slip downstairs and fill my stocking with largesse. I went on making out extravagant lists of wishes, erupting with studied facsimiles of surprise when (imagine!) Santa came through with my fondest desires.

I even continued to put out milk and cookies long past the age of reason, giggling each morning-after when a big toothy bite had appeared amidst the chocolate chips.

I knew, Mom. There was lipstick on the milk glass.

Though I couldn't bear to admit to you that I realized who was munching Santa's snacks in the dead of night, I did try to lighten your burden in my own way. Why else do you suppose I insisted on supplying carrots for his reindeer instead of a mouthful of hay?

The best part was letting you think you'd pulled it off for another year.

Bad news, Mom. I figured out what you and Dad were up to when I was five years old...just big enough to make the connection between the illustrations in the Montgomery Ward holiday catalog and the surprises that showed up wrapped beneath our tree.

If you hadn't done your job so well, belief might have hung suspended for a little longer. But really: How could I not connect Point A with Point B when my heart's desire showed up so dependably on Christmas morning, as faithful as the Post Office — and in the first-choice color, style and size I'd circled?

Popular convention may allow for a Santa who knows when you're sleeping and when you're awake and whether you've been bad or good, but it certainly doesn't leave much room for one who gets catalog numbers right down to the last digit.

As my tiny anklets expanded into ever-larger schoolgirl knee-highs and then, alas, into monstrous pantyhose, I held my silence...even as the care with which they were annually hung by the chimney degenerated into concern that they'd crack the plaster.

But that vow of silence was becoming increasingly strained.

Oh, it wasn't that *I* couldn't keep a secret myself. What made the season ticklish was the need to prevent my little brother Gary — given to blurts — from making some impulsive comment and letting you and Dad know the jig was up.

Not only was I desperate not to ruin the Santa tradition for parents who worked as hard as you to keep it alive; I'd acquired the very strong suspicion that once your deception was unmasked, the secular aspects of Christmas morn would revert to just another date with a bowl of cornflakes — no more, no less.

The uncomfortable urge that this matter be discussed grew more and more pressing as my birthdays added up. Yet I resisted and bludgeoned my brother into relative submission on the issue. Maybe one of the neighborhood kids would reveal to our parents that their fantasies of Santa Claus belonged on the shelf with the bronzed baby shoes, but they'd hear no discouraging words from their own off-spring — not as long as I could cajole, reason or blackmail Gary into agreement.

Did you notice that we both seemed unnaturally slow to debunk the myth that is supposed to signal the end of childhood? Did you worry you were raising two Peter Pans?

I do know you began dropping subtle hints as we marched on toward our teens, like the observation that money does not grow on trees, at least above the Arctic Circle. We'd notice you groaning as we whipped up peanut-butter-and-pickle sandwiches for Santa's traditional late-night snack. If the new pajamas didn't fit, you'd wrap them up to return to Montgomery Ward's — and ask us to mail the package.

Yet how could I confess once I'd stayed silent for so long? If you were still game, the least I could do was play by the time-tested rules.

By then I'd allowed my sixteenth birthday to come and go without admitting that I knew you and Dad were behind the apple, the orange, the handful of peanuts and that fresh copy of my all-time favorite novel, *How the Grinch Stole Christmas* by Dr. Seuss.

How do you tell your mother that, now that you're twenty-one, you'd appreciate it if Santa could leave a bottle of Beefeaters along with the Lifesavers?

This parent understood my love for Grinches. How could I explain to her, even into my mid-20s, that her increasingly perplexed attempts to coax me to sit on Santa's knee and whisper what I wanted into his ear were not only anachronistic ... they were downright dangerous?

Sooner or later it was bound to come to this. Merry Christmas, Mother. Stop stuffing fruit in my hosiery.

Look at the bright side. You need no longer bother to hide the Sears catalog from Columbus Day until New Year's Eve. No more gnawing carrots on behalf of Dasher and Dancer and Prancer and Rudolph. You can have the wall beside the chimney repainted; there will be no more thumbtack holes and dangling socks to mar it.

Thanks. They were good years. My brother and I enjoyed them almost as much, I think, as you and Dad did.

Life post-Santa Claus needn't be lonely, either. Plenty of old friends remain. After all, I haven't said a word about the tooth fairy, have I? Or the Easter bunny. You can keep those carrots for the rabbit if you insist.

And there's always the Grinch. In the Grinch I do still believe, even at a ripening age.

At a moment like this, I know just how he felt.

Nancy Edmonds Hanson: "Mom, I Hate To Tell You This...."
Howard Binford's Guide, 1983.

The Case of the Forbidden Fruit

Janet Letnes Martin

Shirley's Circle had spent the better part of the morning bagging goodies for the Sunday school children. At First Lutheran of the Good Shepherd, it was a tradition to give each child who participated in the Christmas program a bag containing an apple, a variety of nuts — almonds, walnuts, hazels, pecans, peanuts — and a few pieces of hard holiday candy.

The women had organized an assembly line so they could clip along at a good pace. Mrs. Andrew Olson opened the brown paper bags and set them on end. Mrs. G.J. Jensen put two scoops of nuts into each bag. The pastor's wife polished the apples, and Mrs. Lester Olavness put them in the bags. Miss Olive Thorson shoveled in two scoops of candy, and since Mrs. Emil Strandquist was sick, Shirley did double duty. She cut the ribbon that was to be tied around each bag, tied a bow, and then curled the ribbon ends with the edge of a scissors.

"I don't know about you," said Miss Olive Thorson, "but when I was a child, we were a lot more appreciative of the treats the church gave us at Christmas than these kids are. We didn't get as many nuts as they do either."

"It gets worse every year," chimed in Mrs. G.J. Jensen, as she put a scoop of nuts into a bag. "If their attitudes don't change, I think we should just eliminate treats altogether."

"Well," said Shirley, "when I saw four smashed apples outside the church after last year's program, I was thinking the same thing. But, you know, kids nowadays eat apples and nuts for snacks, so this is no special treat for them. Maybe we should just bag them up for the shut-ins instead."

The pastor's wife, who hadn't said much since she came, spoke up. "I think it's a good idea to give some special treats to our shut-ins, but I don't think apples or nuts are very appropriate. Most of them don't have the teeth to handle that kind of food. Maybe we could give them cheese or peach sauce."

Shirley was irked. She was sure none of the women wanted to spend more money on the shut-ins, but no one dared disagree with the pastor's wife. Well, she wasn't about to let that idea stand without comment.

"As far as the shut-ins go, it's the thought that counts," she said, as she continued to cut, tie and curl the ribbon. "Don't expect us to support them."

The pastor and his wife had only been in Heartsberg for two months, and although Shirley knew it was only fair to reserve judgment until they had been in town for at least six, she didn't feel they were the same caliber folk as the previous pastor and his wife. Aunt Wilma had told her many times that liberal seminary training made new, young pastors a different breed. Shirley wasn't sure she completely agreed with that, though. It seemed to her that pastors' wives had changed more than the pastors.

Years ago pastors' wives wouldn't have dreamed of picking out their own wallpaper and paint for the parsonage. They were always satisfied with whatever the church council decided. But this pastor's wife not only dismissed every rule and regulation in the congregational by-laws entitled "The Care and Feeding of the Pastor and His Family." She also let the council know she needed soft water. Can you beat that! Twenty-five years ago, the pastor's wife was just thankful to have running water.

There were other things, too, that didn't set right with Shirley. Not one soul, not even the council members, had been invited to the parsonage for an open house and tour. Miss Olive Thorson had mentioned that she had seen the pastor's wife entertaining her kids with Tic-Tac-Toe and Hangman on the back of the Sunday bulletin in the middle of the pastor's sermon. And others had commented that she talked more about the secular than the sacred things in life.

Shirley was relieved when they finally finished bagging the Sunday school treats, and she felt even better when the pastor's wife said she couldn't come the next day to help fill the food baskets for the shut-ins. One bad apple spoils the whole bunch, she said to herself.

But when the Circle members gathered in the church basement, there wasn't a leftover apple or nut to be found anywhere. "What a shame," lamented Shirley. "I guess the shut-ins will have to be satisfied with cookies this year." But she knew she couldn't be satisfied until she knew all the facts.

When she told Ed about the missing apples and nuts, he said, "It must have been the kids." Shirley was positive he was wrong. She knew kids well enough to realize that if they were going to steal, they'd go for pop or candy. She hated to think the pastor's wife would stoop so low, but her comments questioning the wisdom of giving apples and nuts to the shut-ins made Shirley wonder.

"Aunt Wilma," she said over the phone that evening. "If you had seen the way the pastor's wife looked at the apples when she was polishing them yesterday, you'd have to think she might have pulled an Eve and taken the forbidden fruit. She might be the kind of pastor's wife who thinks that any food left at the church automatically becomes the property of the pastor."

"I've heard there are pastors' wives who feel that way," said Aunt Wilma. "A few years ago one over in Hivdahl got caught taking the pennies out of a birthday bank."

Shirley couldn't wait until the next evening. She and Ed were going to bring a couple of chickens to the parsonage as a Christmas gift for the pastor and his family. In years past, it had just been Ed who delivered them. But since she hadn't seen the parsonage, and it would give her the chance to ask the pastor right in front of his wife if he knew what had happened to the leftover apples and nuts, she made plans to go.

They arrived when the family was eating supper, and Shirley could sense that Ed was uncomfortable and wanted to make it a short visit. So she plunged in. "Pastor, do you know what happened to the leftover apples and nuts?"

"I wasn't even aware there had been any apples or nuts left," he answered.

When Shirley glanced at the pastor's wife to see if she were reacting in a guilty way, her eyes fell on a flowered china bowl in the center of the table.

Waldorf salad. It was so chocked full of apples and nuts she could hear them crunch as the pastor's wife put a forkful into her mouth.

Shirley didn't need any further evidence. "Ed," she said on the way home, "No one serves Waldorf salad for everyday unless they're rich, and even though we pay the pastor pretty well for what he does, it still isn't enough for them to indulge in a salad like that at an ordinary meal."

The next Sunday the pastor's wife and children sat down in the pew ahead of Shirley and Ed. And Shirley knew she'd have a hard time mustering up a polite hello when they shook hands during the Peace. Ed had never felt comfortable shaking hands during the service, and now she knew exactly how he felt.

Shirley was thinking about the missing apples and nuts when the pastor started his sermon — "Give and It Shall Be Given Unto You." But she was jolted back to attention when he began telling a story.

"Last Christmas," he said, "when my family was eating supper, a dirty, tattered man whom I had never seen before, stopped at our house. He was driving a rusty, dilapidated car full of kids. And he asked if he could borrow $2.00 for gas because he was broke and on his way North to try to get work.

"I gave him the money and a bag of groceries," the pastor continued. "And even though he said he'd pay me back, I never expected to hear from him again.

"Well, one night last week as we were having family devotions, there was a knock at the door. There he stood, the same man, carrying a bushel of apples and a big bag of nuts. He had looked long and hard to find our new residence, but he wanted to say thanks for the kindness. He had found a good job and was once again on his feet."

Shirley didn't want to hear any more. She was ashamed. The circumstantial evidence had seemed overwhelming, but it had been wrong, and she had jumped to a petty conclusion.

She felt even more humbled when, during the Peace, the pastor's wife looked her straight in the eyes and said, "My husband found out that when the Luther Leaguers went caroling, they passed out the leftover apples and nuts to the needy."

But the worst sting came from Ed. He gave her a "see-I-didn't-figure-you-were-right" nudge and then whispered, "Didn't I tell you it was the kids?"

Janet Letnes Martin: "The Case of the Forbidden Fruit."
From *Whodunit?* Martin House Publications, 1988.

A Merrie Prairie Christmas

The Spirit of St. Nick

Otto J. Boutin

Big Mike was quite a guy, with broad shoulders and a jagged scar across his cheek. He was the best working foreman that ever ran the composing room of the *Michigan Daily Gazette.*

The boys had always given him a half gallon of bourbon for Christmas, but this year Big Mike presented a problem. He admitted he had gone on the wagon. And he didn't want cigars. He intended to quit smoking.

So here it was, six o'clock on Christmas Eve and we still didn't know what to give Big Mike. The boys had pitched in their money and expected me to go out among the last-minute shoppers to buy a present.

I was on my way when Red Ralph tapped me on the shoulder. Red Ralph was a Lino operator, quite balmy, as most of them are.

"Big Mike likes women," he pointed out in his rasping voice. "Let's give him a blonde."

"A what?"

"A blonde manikin. I bought her at an auction sale. I've got her in the car."

With misgivings, I went with Ralph to the parking lot and helped him get the blonde manikin. He had kept her wrapped in a blanket in the trunk of his car because he couldn't gather the nerve to bring her home to his wife and six kids, even if she were a bargain at ten dollars. She still wore the long, black nightgown she had been modeling.

When Big Mike stood at the Christmas tree, waiting for his present, we told him to close his eyes. Then we shoved the manikin into his arms.

"Meet Lulu," we said. "She's yours." Big Mike blushed. Then, like Errol Flynn, he picked her up and carried her across the shop.

"I'll keep Lulu in the utility room," he said. "She'll be our mascot."

The utility room, decorated with mops, pails and brooms, also contained a cot where a person could catch forty winks between editions.

Big Mike stopped at the door and peered into the darkness. "The place is occupied," he said. "The janitor is sleeping off a hangover."

Sure enough, there was The Duke, snoring in oblivion, with an army blanket pulled up to his gaunt chin. His feet were sticking out over the edge of the cot.

Big Mike leaned the manikin against the wall, careful not to disturb the sleeping janitor.

"Snuggle her up to the Duke," someone said. "Give the bachelor a thrill for Christmas."

The Duke, sweetly dreaming in his celibacy, turned his back on Lulu and kept snoring in a higher key.

Big Mike walked with me into the brittle night of sparkling stars. The streets were deserted. People were at home, eating, drinking, exchanging junk.

"The trouble with a reputation," Big Mike was saying, "is that you have to live up to it. I stopped drinking years ago, but the fellows kept bringing me bourbon. I stopped smoking long ago, but I still had to keep chewing the stub of a cigar. It was a symbol of authority. And, of course, I've stopped chasing women, but everybody thinks I'm still wild about dolls. Nobody really knows me. They know my reputation, but not me. I'll bet you don't know where I'm going right now."

"Where?" I asked.

"Salvation Army. Sing a few songs with my kind of people. We'll get doughnuts and coffee. Maybe cake."

As Big Mike sang "The Rock of Ages" in his deep baritone, I realized that there is in every man a secret soul that only God knows about. I thought I saw a halo around my companion's head as we walked to his house.

His mother-in-law, built like a Japanese wrestler, met us on the stairs. "Where the hell yuh been?" she demanded, arms akimbo. "Horsing around at some Christmas party?"

Big Mike, the undisputed boss of a dozen men, stood as meek as an unwanted dog.

"Your wife is out looking for you," shouted the Japanese wrestler, trying to make herself heard over the coarse laughter coming from the house. "She's ready to kill."

Shoulders sagging, Big Mike turned away. Silently we walked the streets, with no destination in mind. Before we know it we were back at the *Michigan Daily Gazette.*

Something had happened at the newspaper plant. Squad cars were converging from all directions. Policemen, with drawn revolvers, were storming the stairs. We ran along with them.

We stopped at the door to the utility closet. The beams of three flashlights were focused on the cot.

The Duke was still asleep, a big purple bump on his forehead. Lulu lay beside him, one of her beautiful legs dangling from under the blanket.

Her contours were provocative, but her face was a mess. Her jawbone, unattached, was on the floor. Her beautiful blue eyes lay like marbles on each side of her, staring into opposite directions, quite far away from her painted eyebrows. Her skull was shattered into fragments of deathly white chalk. A 25-pound bar of type metal lay across her crushed nose.

Somebody gave oxygen to The Duke. Sputtering he rose to his enormous height.

"What happened?" the police sergeant asked him. "I dunno," mumbled The Duke, caressing the purple egg on his forehead.

"Who's the doll?" asked the sergeant. The Duke groggily stared at Lulu. "Beats the hell outa me," he answered.

"Is your name Mike?" the sergeant continued.

"No. Mike is over there."

Solemnly we removed our hats as a policeman pulled a blanket over Lulu's smashed face.

"It's a helluva practical joke," the sergeant grumbled to Mike. "Your wife came down here looking for you. She thought she caught you making out with the blonde. So she let both of you have it across the head with that big bar of lead. When she heard the skull crack she ran to the station to give herself up. Kinda hysterical. She's in a cell now, on her knees, praying."

Big Mike grinned. "'Let her pray," he said. "Praying is good for the soul. Especially on Christmas."

Otto J. Boutin: "The Spirit of St. Nick." From *A Catfish in the Bodoni*. North Star Press: 1970.

The Truth About Santa Claus

Ruth Tweed

Audrey Benson was a big-eyed little girl with a normal amount of childish curiosity. She must have out-questioned the adults in her life because by the time she was six and a half she felt it was safer to keep her questions to herself and come to her own conclusions. One didn't get laughed at that way. There were some things that were unanswerable and she still did quite a bit of pondering over them. She couldn't understand why her parents were so eager to have a house of their own. They talked about it all the time. There was nothing wrong with the house they lived in, upstairs at Mrs. Lundquist's. In fact, it was a dandy house. None of her friends could go upstairs on the outside of the house, run through their living quarters and down another stairway on the inside. She had learned without being told that they could do that only when Mrs. Lundquist was away.

She also wondered why her dad worried about the School Board. When she started school she looked around to see if there was some special board but couldn't find any. She was sure she'd find it someday.

Around Christmas time she wondered about Santa Claus. There were so many things that didn't make sense — like who tattled to Santa when they were bad and why naughty kids got things anyway. If Santa was good and kind why didn't the poor kids get anything? Her mother used to help pack Christmas baskets for the poor people — why couldn't Santa take care of that? She tried to talk to her little sister Faye about it, but Faye was a true believer and wasn't about to question a good thing when she had it.

Santa Claus always came to town early in December. The children went to a free movie in the fire hall and then Santa would pass out bags of candy and some of the bravest children would climb on his lap and tell him what they wanted for Christmas. Faye was too shy and Audrey herself was never bold enough to climb on his knee but she dared shake his hand and tell him what they wanted for Christmas. He laughed a jolly "ho ho" and said he'd do his best if they'd been good and, of course, they had. Even Mrs. Lundquist said so and she was kind of crabby sometimes. The year before Santa had brought them the sled they asked for the this year they planned to request the toy kitchen they had seen in the Sears Roebuck catalog. Audrey had memorized the page number to make sure he made no mistake. She thought it would be fun to surprise her mother so she said they were going to ask for new dolls. She knew Santa didn't approve of lying but this wasn't a lie when it was to protect a secret.

The family always stayed home for Christmas. Mrs. Benson was the church organist so was busy with Sunday School programs and choir practice right up to the last minute. Mr. Benson, who was the school principal, history teacher and basketball coach, seldom had a free evening to spend with his family. Mrs. Lundquist often looked after the children when their parents were at school or church. The girls could hardly wait until Christmas morning when they'd have their mother and dad to themselves.

Christmas mornings were always the same. They would have opened some of their gifts from relatives on Christmas Eve, but the Santa Claus gifts were left for morning. They'd look in their stockings first and find some small toys and cookies that looked like their mother's and some candies like Mrs. Lundquist made. Then there would be the big packages under the tree and that was the exciting part. The year they expected the kitchen they could hardly go to sleep thinking about it. When they got to the Christmas tree they could see that the two big packages just weren't big enough for all the kitchen things.

Their dolls were beautiful. Audrey thought they were the prettiest dolls she had ever seen, but she was disappointed in Santa — he had sounded so positive when she had told him about the kitchen. Maybe it was her own fault for fibbing to her mother. Perhaps Mrs. Lundquist had something to do with it. She brought up two little suitcases filled with clothes she had made for the dolls. They fit perfectly so she must have known about it. By afternoon both girls loved their dolls and decided they'd get the kitchen next year.

Every year they spent part of Christmas vacation with their grandparents in Minneapolis. They had a house almost as big as Mrs. Lundquist's and their grandma let them run and bounce balls and make all the noise they pleased. Audrey's mother complained that they were being spoiled but her dad said that once a year didn't hurt anybody.

Sometimes their cousin Sheila came over to play with them. She was Audrey's age but quite a bit bigger so there was always a box of out-grown clothes for Audrey. She liked getting the things, but got tired of hearing Sheila brag about it, especially when she'd strut around, showing off her *new* things. Once Sheila had been especially obnoxious and Audrey had lost her temper and punched her in the stomach.

Aunt Connie, Sheila's mother, had invited all of them over for dinner on New Year's Day. The girls were dressed in the red velvet dresses their grandmother had made for them and dressed their dolls in their best finery. Sheila would be impressed.

Sheila met them at the door. She was wearing a swishy blue taffeta dress and carried a doll that was almost as big as she was, also wearing a swishy blue taffeta dress. Sheila spun around to show the skirt and said, "We've got coats alike too. Audrey can have my old one. It has two buttons missing."

Audrey had promised not to fight with Sheila. She clenched her teeth and clutched her doll.

After dinner the girls went upstairs to play in Sheila's room. She said Santa had brought her something they had to see. There it was — *their* kitchen was set up in Sheila's room. Santa had made a dreadful mistake!

"That's what Audrey and I wanted," Faye blurted, "but we got our dolls instead."

"Is that *all* you got? I suppose it's because you're poor and Santa never brings much to poor people."

Fireworks exploded in Audrey's head. For the second time in her life she punched Sheila in the stomach. Sheila screamed, Faye cried, and the grown-ups came running.

"She hit me. She's jealous of my kitchen," Sheila yelled.

"Audrey, I'm ashamed," scolded Mother.

The incident was soon forgotten by Faye and Sheila who played with the kitchen all afternoon. Sheila was on her best behavior from then on and let Faye turn on the water in the little sink and wash her best doll dishes. Audrey was made to sit with the grown-ups. She hugged her doll and pondered on the injustice of it all. No one had asked for her side of the story. Why did Sheila say they were poor? Arlene, in her class in school, was poor — everybody said so. The only Christmas gifts she got were in the basket from church. She was always good — a lot nicer than Sheila. Once Sheila had tipped the garbage can and told Aunt Connie the neighbor boy did it. Last summer when they came for a visit she called Mrs. Lundquist an ugly old lady and stuck her tongue out at the minister. Still Santa always brought her lots of presents!

Faye and Audrey talked it over and Audrey decided that it wasn't worth trying any more. She didn't care what Santa thought of her. Faye was scared and begged her not to talk that way.

The next year Faye started first grade. She and Audrey were proud when they met their daddy in the hall on his way to the high school rooms upstairs.

One day Georgie Johnson said, "There goes the Warden. That's what my brother calls him."

Nobody called Audrey's daddy names and got by with it. She doubled her fist and hit him right in the middle of his fat stomach. He let out a whoop and she socked him in the nose. Blood spurted.

There must have been some kind of rule about the principal's daughter not getting into fights. There was a lot of commotion and

A Merrie Prairie Christmas

Audrey was sent home in disgrace. Her father said something about Mr. Johnson being president of the School Board. Mrs. Lundquist said she wished she'd seen it because the Johnson boys were all a bunch of pests. Later she told them that Mrs. Johnson wanted to call the school but Mr. Johnson said it was a disgrace for his boy to be beaten up by a girl and to forget the whole thing.

Georgie didn't forget it. He got Audrey into trouble every time he could. Her dad told her he didn't care if the kids called him the Warden. High school kids often called the teachers funny names. High school kids were almost grown-up. Audrey thought. It didn't make sense at all. *She* couldn't even call Georgie "Fatty" without getting into trouble.

That year was a hard one for the Bensons. Faye broke her arm and had to be in the hospital. They all had the flu and Mr. Benson missed a week of school. The substitute's salary had to be taken from his unbelievably low pay check. Audrey heard her mother say there wouldn't be much Christmas. Christmas was Christmas, wasn't it? She didn't understand. Maybe Santa — but it was too late to ask him after all the things she'd said about him. Anyway, if they were poor he wouldn't come. He didn't seem to like poor people.

Nobody mentioned the coming trip to Minneapolis until Audrey heard her mother tell Mrs. Lundquist they weren't going. "We can't go without new tires and with the doctor bills and everything we can't buy them now," she explained.

"Why don't you ask for your salary early? Our last organist always did before Christmas."

Audrey hadn't known her mother got paid for playing the organ. "I already did," she answered. "I used it for Christmas presents. Faye told me they wanted a toy kitchen like their cousin Sheila's so I ordered it. I meant to ask you if we could hide it in your apartment."

"Of course," answered Mrs. Lundquist. "It'll be fun. I can't wait to see them with it! They're such darlings."

So that was it! Santa didn't bring the presents — Mother and Daddy bought them with their own money and they did it because they loved them. She giggled to herself. This would be her secret until Faye got bigger. They wouldn't tell Mother. There was no use disappointing her.

The girls kept up the game for a couple years until it was understood that they were too grown-up for Santa. Nobody ever really told them.

Forty years later Audrey was standing in line at a big department store, holding six-year-old Shannon's hand, waiting for Santa Claus.

Shannon was a big-eyed child with a normal curiosity who had out-questioned all the grown-ups in her life until she knew all the answers. Her mother, who was Audrey's daughter, was at work and had asked Audrey to take the child to see Santa.

"You never told us much about Santa," Pam complained. "I think we missed some fun. I want Shannon to know all about Santa — all the magic and surprise." Of course, that meant that Grandma had to cooperate.

Shannon climbed on Santa's knee and chattered happily. She wanted everything in the toy department plus a pony. He laughed and said he'd do his best and now other children were waiting to talk to him. Shannon turned to give him a kiss, then jumped down quickly. Her barrette caught in Santa's beard, and to the horror of the waiting crowd, came along as Shannon hopped down from the glittering pedestal.

Audrey untangled the beard, returned it to the pink-chinned young man and left as quickly as possible. Shannon skipped alongside of her, unconcerned, until they got to the car.

"You know, Grandma," she said in a confidential tone, "I don't think we'd better tell Mommy about this. She still thinks I believe all that stuff."

Ruth Tweed: "The Truth About Christmas." Reprinted with permission from *The Crazy Quilt.*

Santa Claus, Inc.

Robert Karolevitz

> *I think the kids*
> *Will all agree*
> *That Santa needs*
> *No help from me.*

Sometimes I don't think my wife Phyllis has enough faith in my ability to get things done.

For instance, just before Christmas she said, "It's a blessing you're not Santa Claus, or a lot of little kids would be in for a very disappointing holiday."

"And just what do you mean by that?" I asked in my most St. Nicholasly tone.

"Well, for openers," she replied, "you'd never get the reindeer hitched up right, and you'd probably forget all their names."

"I would not," I argued. "Who could ever forget Donder and Blitzen and Vixen and Claude?"

Then I told her I'd probably let Rudolph ride in the back of the sleigh so I could use his nose as a tail light. After all, I wouldn't want to get rear-ended by some high-soaring Christmas Eve party-goer.

Deliveries Guaranteed Before Easter

She disregarded my attempt at humor and went on: "Since you don't like to fly, I can just see you now, getting Dasher and Dancer and Cupid and Claude hung up on the Santa Ana Freeway or at the stop-light at Fourth and Broadway."

I tried to explain to her that they'd probably have to overlook the 55-mile-an-hour speed limit for one night if I was to get my job done, but she wasn't even listening.

"What bothers me most," she persisted, "are all those plaintive letters from eager youngsters scattered all over the globe. The way you keep your office, you'd have them so mixed up that you'd never get the deliveries straight!"

I tried not to let her remarks irritate me as I quipped: "Did you know that Santa's name is really Clausewicz and that I might be related to him? He's North POLISH, you know!"

Apparently she didn't think that was the least bit funny because she kept right on with her uncomplimentary theme.

"I don't know how you'd ever find a little boy in Schenectady or an anxious little girl in Tanganyika when you get lost between here and the barn." she ranted on.

"Besides that, you're always late, and coming down somebody's chimney on St. Patrick's Day eve could get you in a whole lot of trouble!"

I'd Be Sooted for the Job

I chuckled at that particular Irish barb (which was pretty good for a Norwegian), and as I did, I noticed that my little belly shook like a bowl full of Schmucker's best.

"Speaking of chimneys," she continued. "you'd probably get stuck in the first flue you came to, and they wouldn't find you 'til Easter."

I didn't know how we got on this dumb subject in the first place, but I was beginning to get a little hot under the white fur collar of my red suit. I decided it was time to set her straight.

"In the first place," I struck back (and my eyes didn't twinkle and my dimples weren't merry), "I'd never run the place in that antiquated old way."

"All my elves would be computer programmers, and they'd have every kid who was naughty or nice on a floppy disc, their letters would be in the memory bank and I'd have deliveries scheduled on a print-out which would guarantee better overnight service than Purolator."

Christmas is Too Seasonal

"Secondly, I'd move the whole operation to Sun City because it's ridiculous to work out of all those snow drifts up North. I'd retire Prancer and Comet and Claude to a comfortable reindeer pasture and contract with UPS for distribution.

"I might even consider diversifying and take over Mother's Day, Father's Day and Thanksgiving. I'd incorporate and maybe go into the fast food business, too. Reindeer burgers are out, of course."

Phyllis softened noticeably as I defended my honor. But I had one more thing to add (laying a finger aside of my nose as I did): "The world may not be ready for a crew-cut Santa Claus with all of the foibles you've just described, but there is one job I can do just as well as that jolly old elf himself – and that is to exclaim:

"Happy Christmas to all, and to all a good night!"

Robert Karolevitz: "Santa Claus, Inc." From *Toulouse the Goose and Other Ridiculous Stories*, a collection of columns by Bob Karolevitz, Dakota Homestead Publishers.